WAR!

"Well, if you ask me, your story about *our* slumber party backfired."

Jana slammed down the phone in Beth's ear, but now it was Beth's turn to be angry. How could Jana blame me? How could she possibly think it was my fault that Laura McCall was making fools out of us? she thought desperately. How could anybody think that? It wasn't fair.

Beth stomped back to her room, grabbed the pillow off her bed and hurled it onto the floor. Her life had turned into a roller coaster ride: up one minute, and in the pits the next—and it was all because of Laura. Beth would get her for this if it was the last thing she ever did.

"Watch out, Laura McCall," she muttered under her breath. "From now on, it's all-out war!"

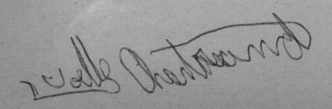

Bantam Skylark Books by Betsy Haynes
Ask your bookseller for the books you have missed

THE AGAINST TAFFY SINCLAIR CLUB
TAFFY SINCLAIR STRIKES AGAIN
TAFFY SINCLAIR, QUEEN OF THE SOAPS
TAFFY SINCLAIR AND THE ROMANCE
  MACHINE DISASTER
BLACKMAILED BY TAFFY SINCLAIR
TAFFY SINCLAIR, BABY ASHLEY, AND ME
TAFFY SINCLAIR AND THE MELANIE MAKE-
  OVER
THE TRUTH ABOUT TAFFY SINCLAIR
THE GREAT MOM SWAP
THE GREAT BOYFRIEND TRAP

Books in The Fabulous Five Series

#1 SEVENTH-GRADE RUMORS
#2 THE TROUBLE WITH FLIRTING
#3 THE POPULARITY TRAP
#4 HER HONOR, KATIE SHANNON
#5 THE BRAGGING WAR

THE FABULOUS FIVE

The Bragging War

Betsy Haynes

A BANTAM SKYLARK BOOK®
TORONTO · NEW YORK · LONDON · SYDNEY · AUCKLAND

RL 5, 009-012

THE BRAGGING WAR
A Bantam Skylark Book/February 1989

*Skylark Books is a registered trademark of Bantam Books, a division
of Bantam Doubleday Dell Publishing Group, Inc. Registered in
U.S. Patent and Trademark Office and elsewhere.*

ISBN 0-553-15651-9

Published simultaneously in the United States and Canada

---

*Bantam Books are published by Bantam Books, a division of Bantam
Doubleday Dell Publishing Group, Inc. Its trademark, consisting of
the words "Bantam Books" and the portrayal of a rooster, is Regis-
tered in U.S. Patent and Trademark Office and in other countries.
Marca Registrada. Bantam Books, 666 Fifth Avenue, New York,
New York 10103.*

PRINTED IN THE UNITED STATES OF AMERICA

S   0 9 8 7 6 5 4 3 2 1

The Bragging War

CHAPTER

1

*B*eth Barry put the cap back on the toothpaste tube and grinned widely at herself in the bathroom mirror.

"Ah," she whispered. "The face of a star! Movies? Television? The stage? Maybe I'll do the very first variety show ever televised from outer space." She giggled and picked up her hairbrush, holding it up like a microphone and animating her words with exaggerated gestures like ones she had seen on television. "Good evening, ladies and gentlemen. This is Beth Barry coming to you *live*—from the MOON!"

She started to break into song and a dance step but stopped, letting the hand holding the hairbrush drift downward to rest on the sink again. Then she leaned forward until her nose almost touched the mirror.

"The mouth," she grumbled as she frowned at her own reflection. "My eyes and nose are okay, but why do I have to have such a big mouth? It's huge! It's terrible! It's gross! How can I ever become a star with a mouth like that?"

"Beth! Will you get out of the bathroom and give someone else a chance!" bellowed her older brother Brian from the hall. "You're going to make me late for school."

She gave herself one last appraising look in the mirror, pinched her mouth together with a thumb and forefinger to make it look smaller, and then hurried to her room to get her books, stopping only long enough to make a gruesome face at Brian.

Her mouth was still on her mind when she got to Wakeman Junior High, or Wacko Junior High as most kids called it, and she hurried to the special spot by the fence where she always met her four best friends before school in the morning.

Their clique was called The Fabulous Five, and they had been close friends since early in grade school in spite of the fact that their personalities were very different. Jana Morgan was the unofficial leader, and whenever the group had trouble with Taffy Sinclair or their rivals, The Fantastic Foursome, she was usually the one with the cool head. Melanie Edwards had gotten carried away with getting thin and pretty last year in sixth grade, and now she was totally boy crazy. At one time Melanie had thought she was in love with Scott Daly, Shane Arrington, and Garrett Boldt—all at once. Christie Winchell was smart and popular, and she definitely wouldn't let anyone push her around. And then there was Katie Shannon, who wanted to be a lawyer when she grew up and defend women from the injustices of the world. She was even one of the judges on Wacko's new Teen Court.

It was Katie who spoke up first when Beth reached them and popped the question about whether or not her mouth was too big.

"Well, sometimes it is," Katie said seriously. "But most people know not to pay too much attention to what you say. You're just being dramatic most of the time."

Beth looked at her in stunned silence for a moment and then burst out, "I'm not talking about what I *say*! This is serious. I'm talking about the size. You know," she implored. "Does it spoil my looks?"

"I don't think it's too big," offered Jana. "It fits your face. You wouldn't be Beth Barry if it were different."

"Thanks, Jana," Beth said, and then sighed. "You're a super friend, but what I really want to know is whether or not you think my mouth will spoil my chances of becoming an actress."

Melanie giggled. "Not if you get to play parts where you do a lot of kissing!"

Everyone broke up at that. Even Beth.

"Come on, guys. Cut the comedy," said Christie. "It's almost time for the bell."

Beth pursed her lips and headed toward the front door of the school with her four friends. When they passed the gum tree, she stopped and slapped a pink wad of watermelon bubble gum onto an empty space on the bark. The old oak tree was dotted with chewing gum of every color in the rainbow because Mr. Bell, the principal, absolutely loathed gum in class. The students had decided that the oak tree was the perfect place to leave their gum before entering the building every morning.

Melanie wrinkled her nose. "That tree is gross," she muttered.

"Not as gross as what I see over there," said Jana, pointing to a small crowd of girls that was gathering on the sidewalk near the door.

Beth glanced toward the crowd. In the center stood The Fantastic Foursome, the rival clique that had come to Wacko Junior High from Riverfield Elementary School. Laura McCall was their leader, and she was the one everyone else was listening to. She was tall and pretty with a long braid that started at the top of her head and reached all the way to her waist. Now as she talked, she wore a superior look on her face and flicked the end of her braid back and forth with one hand like a cat flicks its tail. Beside her stood tiny, black-haired Tammy Lucero, whom everyone knew loved to talk. Beth could see by the way she was bouncing up and down that she was dying to get a word in. Beside Tammy was blond, prissy Melissa McConnell, who was a perfectionist with a capital *P.* Last was Funny Hawthorne, smiling, as usual. Some people thought she was a bubblehead because she laughed at practically everything, but Beth knew that Jana believed she was just a nice girl with a great sense of humor.

"What do you think Laura and her crowd are up to now?" asked Melanie.

"I don't know," said Beth, "but if you ask me, we'd better find out. They might be spreading rumors about us."

"I agree," said Jana. "That seems to be their favorite thing to do."

"Or maybe Laura's bragging again," said Christie. "She thinks it's such a big deal that her parents are divorced and she lives with her father. She just loves to go around telling everyone about how she has him wrapped around her little finger and can get away with absolutely anything."

Beth and her friends moved closer until they were only a few feet away and definitely close enough to hear what Laura was saying. Christie had been right.

"And that's not all," Laura was boasting. "My dad

let me take his new red Maserati out all by myself."

"Do you mean that you *drove* it?" Alexis Duvall asked incredulously.

What? thought Beth. Laura has to be kidding.

She glanced at her four friends and they all looked as if they didn't believe Laura's big story either.

"Of course," replied Laura, tilting her chin upward. "My dad lets me do anything I want to. He even said that next time I can give my friends a ride." Tammy, Melissa, and Funny were nodding in agreement.

"But you're only thirteen," said Gloria Drexler. "You don't have a driver's license!"

"So?" said Laura. "My dad knows I'm a good driver."

"But what if a policeman stops you?" Mona Vaughn asked in an excited voice. "It's against the law to drive a car without a license. It wouldn't matter that your dad let you do it."

Laura chuckled. "That's what you think. My dad knows the police chief and most of the officers. They wouldn't give *me* a ticket."

Laura shot a haughty look in the direction of The Fabulous Five and then flipped her braid over her shoulder and strolled confidently toward the school. Her three friends followed her, but so did several other girls, including some from Mark Twain Elementary, The Fabulous Five's old school. Every single one of them was chattering and trying to get Laura's attention.

"Will you look at that!" cried Beth. "There go Alexis and Sara and Kim. They actually *believed* her."

"That liar!" Katie spat out the words.

"Right!" said Jana. "I don't care if her father does let her get away with murder. No parent would let a seventh-grader take the car all by herself. I don't care how many policemen he knows. How could those kids fall for a phony story like that?"

"I don't know either," said Melanie. "But they certainly did. Just look at them. They're tripping over their feet to talk to her."

"Yeah," said Christie. "Alexis and Kim and Sara are supposed to be our friends, not hers."

"Don't you get it?" said Katie. "She's doing that on purpose. She wants everybody to think that The Fantastic Foursome are really big deals and The Fabulous Five are a bunch of losers."

Beth narrowed her eyes as she watched Laura lead the group of adoring girls into the building. It was disgusting. They couldn't let Laura get away with a thing like that.

CHAPTER

2

"Somebody think of a way to get back at Laura McCall," ordered Beth, kicking a rock through the grass as she and the rest of The Fabulous Five headed for their place by the fence after lunch.

She had had a terrible morning. First her boyfriend, Keith Masterson, had stopped her in the hall between classes to ask if she had heard about Laura's getting to drive her father's car. He had gone on and on about Laura until Beth had wanted to throw up.

What if Keith decided he liked Laura now instead of her because of Laura's bragging? The Barry family car was an ancient van that was big enough to hold two parents, five kids, and a gigantic old English sheepdog. It was dented, rusted, and full of dog hair. She could never compete with a snazzy little red Maserati in a car like that.

Then, to make matters worse, in every single class she saw girls whispering among themselves and heard the words "Maserati," "driving," and "Laura McCall." It had burned her up just to think about how Laura was impressing the socks off everybody with her phony story, but so far, she hadn't been able to come up with a way to get even.

"I've been trying hard to think of something," said Christie. "But who can top a story like hers?"

"And did you see the way everybody was crowding around her in the cafeteria just now?" asked Jana. "I don't think any of our old friends from Mark Twain Elementary even so much as looked our way. They were too busy buttering up Laura."

"It wasn't just the girls who were buttering her up, either," said Beth. "There were plenty of boys trying to get her attention, too. I saw Keith in the halls this morning, and all he could talk about was Laura McCall."

"Thank goodness I didn't see Randy hanging around her," said Jana. "But I'll admit there were lots of other Mark Twain boys trying to crowd in at her table."

"They all probably think she'll take them for a ride in her father's sports car," grumbled Melanie.

"Big deal!" said Katie, rolling her eyes toward the sky.

"You bet it's a big deal," said Beth. "I can't stand it when somebody tries to make The Fabulous Five look like losers, especially to the boys."

"Hey, guys. Look. Over by the bike rack," said Jana.

Beth glanced around and saw Alexis Duvall and Lisa Snow. They had gone to Mark Twain Elementary with The Fabulous Five and were good friends of Beth and the others. Now they were talking excitedly, and Lisa was bouncing on the balls of her feet.

"Let's go see what's up," said Beth. "I could use some good news."

Beth led her four friends toward Alexis and Lisa, but the instant The Fabulous Five were within earshot of the two girls, both stopped talking and guarded expressions appeared on their faces.

"What's so exciting?" asked Melanie.

"Yeah?" said Christie. "You two look as if you just heard something juicy."

Lisa exchanged nervous glances with Alexis. "Oh, nothing," she said, and shrugged. "We were just acting silly."

"Come on, guys," insisted Beth. "You were excited about something. Are you going to tell us, or not?"

Alexis lifted her chin. "Okay," she said. "I'll tell you. Laura McCall is having a slumber party Friday night, and she just invited both of us."

"What's so great about that?" asked Katie. "Slumber parties are fun, but they're no big deal."

"Well, this one is," Lisa assured them. "Laura said that her father will be out of town and that Mrs. Skinner, the lady that stays with her, is hard of hearing."

Alexis cut in. "Not only that—but Laura said that Mrs. Skinner goes to bed early, and as soon as she goes to her room, we're going to sneak out and do something that will be a *real blast*." She looked at Lisa again, and when their eyes met, both girls started giggling.

Beth had a sinking feeling. Oh, no, she thought. Laura is at it again. Just like the time she had the party and invited the boyfriends of The Fabulous Five and didn't invite them. "So what is this 'real blast' thing you're going to do?" she asked angrily.

Lisa turned to Beth. Mirth was shining in Lisa's eyes, and the more she tried to stop laughing, the more little giggles burst out. "Sorry," she said finally. "Laura swore us to secrecy."

"Anybody who tells the secret plan gets the ax," said Alexis. Then the smile left her face and she looked at The Fabulous Five solemnly. "Honest. You guys know that we would tell you if we could."

"Sure," muttered Beth, stomping off toward the school. She couldn't remember when she'd felt so angry. When she got almost to the building, she turned and yelled as loud as she could. "AND THE

MOON IS MADE OUT OF GREEN CHEESE, TOO!"

"Wow," said Jana as she and the others caught up with Beth. "You really let them have it."

"'We'd tell you if we could. Honest,'" Beth mimicked in a high-pitched voice. "I'll *bet* they would," she added sarcastically. "They used to be our friends, but now Laura is wrapping them around her little finger the same as she's done with her dad."

Melanie nodded. "In fact, she's probably started giving them orders and making them do things to be friends with her just the way she does with Tammy, Melissa, and Funny. Pretty soon it will probably be The Fantastic Six or The Fantastic Seven."

"Yuck," said Christie. "There are too many of them already."

"Wait a minute," Beth said slowly. An idea was forming in her mind. "I've got a great idea!" she shouted as her spirits began to soar. "*We'll* have a slumber party the same night as Laura's. In fact, we can have it at my house. And we'll ask everybody that Laura might ask, only we'll get to them before she does."

"How do you know we can do that?" asked Christie. "Maybe she's already asked everybody."

"You could tell from the way Alexis and Lisa were acting that Laura had just asked them," said Jana. "I doubt if she's had time to get to everyone. I think Beth has a good idea."

"Me, too," said Melanie. "But are you sure that your parents will let you have a slumber party?"

"Sure," said Beth, sounding more confident than she felt. Being the middle child of five made it hard to get her parents' attention most of the time, much less to get them to agree to disrupting the family's weekend with a huge slumber party. Still, there wasn't time to check it out first.

"Hey," shouted Katie. "Here come Kim and Sara. Let's grab them before Laura gets them in her clutches."

The Fabulous Five made a beeline for Kim Baxter and Sara Sawyer, who were just coming out the cafeteria door and onto the school ground. Like Alexis and Lisa, they were old friends from Mark Twain and had always been loyal to their former schoolmates. They were talking quietly to each other. Good, thought Beth. They aren't as excited as Alexis and Lisa. Laura probably hasn't gotten to them yet.

"Hi," Beth said brightly as she and her friends came to a stop directly in Kim and Sara's path. "I'm going to have a slumber party Friday night. Can you two come?"

Kim and Sara looked at each other solemnly. "Gosh," said Sara. "We'd love to . . . except . . ." Her voice trailed off and she looked down at her feet.

"Except what?" demanded Beth. When they

didn't answer instantly, she went on in a sarcastic voice, "Except that *Lau-RA* asked you first. Is that it?"

"Beth. Knock it off," said Jana, tugging at Beth's shirtsleeve.

Beth ignored her best friend. "What did she promise you? A ride in her dad's sports car?"

Sara put her hands on her hips and faced Beth angrily. "We would have come to your party if you'd asked us first, but you didn't. And I'm glad now. Laura's party is going to be a blast, and she's not a total *grouch* like you are."

Kim nodded her agreement, and the two spun around and marched off in the opposite direction.

Beth groaned. "I blew that, didn't I?" Nobody answered, but she knew that they all agreed. "I'm sorry. It's just that Laura McCall makes me so mad. Who does she think she is anyway, always trying to steal our friends and make us look bad?"

"Forget it," said Katie. "Isn't that Gloria Drexler and Marcie Bee over by the corner of the building? Surely Laura hasn't already asked them."

But Laura had. Beth had trouble controlling herself again when Marcie said, "And is it ever going to be fun. Laura made us promise that we wouldn't tell anyone what we're going to do, but I'll tell you one thing. I can't wait!"

Just as she had heard about Laura all morning, all through afternoon classes Beth caught snatches of conversations between girls who had been invited to Laura's slumber party. Laura had invited girls from Mark Twain Elementary, from Riverfield, and also from Copper Beach. And what was worse, all of them were bursting with excitement.

When The Fabulous Five met at their lockers after school, no one had any good news.

"Even Taffy Sinclair is going to Laura's slumber party," said Melanie. Taffy had been the snottiest girl at Mark Twain, and hardly anyone had gotten along with her. The Fabulous Five had even had a club against her. Of course, she had had one against them, too.

"So is Mona Vaughn," said Christie. "I asked her in social studies class. She said she was really sorry, but she had already promised Laura and she couldn't back out. Do you guys realize that *we'll be the only ones not there?*"

"That's it!" cried Beth.

"What's *it?*" Jana asked sarcastically.

Beth raised an eyebrow and smiled. "If Laura can brag about what's going to happen at her party, so can we. We'll make our party sound so exciting that everyone who is going to hers will back out and come to ours."

"And just how are we going to do that?" asked Melanie. "How can we top hers when we don't even know what she has planned?"

"Leave everything to me," ordered Beth. Even

though she didn't have any idea how she would top Laura's party, her mind was racing. That wacky English rock group Brain Damage would be here in concert next weekend, but there was no rock concert in town this weekend that Laura could be taking them to. No other big events, either. And Alexis and Lisa had mentioned that it was something they were going to do after Mrs. Skinner fell asleep. Was she really going to take all of them for a ride in her father's tiny Maserati? *Practically every girl in the seventh grade?* And what could she come up with so that The Fabulous Five could outdo The Fantastic Foursome and Laura McCall?

CHAPTER

3

*A*ll the way home from school Beth rehearsed what she would say to her parents to persuade them to let her have a slumber party Friday night. She would have to start with that and work on a great plan as she went along. If she or her friends thought of a really terrific way to lure girls away from Laura's party, there could be a real crowd. I'll have to deal with that problem later, she thought.

A bigger problem was going to be getting her parents to listen to her request in the first place. Especially since she didn't know how many people would be coming. With five kids in the family it was always a total madhouse around the Barry household.

At least Todd, her younger brother who was in

the fifth grade, was shooting hoops in the driveway when she got home. That eliminates one distraction, she thought. She waved to him and ducked in the door beside the garage as he tried to blast her with the basketball.

"Hey. Wanna play bombardment?" he shouted as she closed the door.

Inside, her older brother Brian's stereo was cranked up so high that the walls seemed to pulse with the music. Brian was probably upstairs in his room—where he could hear the music better, she thought wryly.

Looking around the family room, she saw that both of her sisters were in their usual afternoon spots. Alicia, the five-year-old, was stretched out on her stomach watching *Sesame Street* with Agatha, the sheepdog, who was stretched out on her stomach, too. As usual, sixteen-year-old Brittany was talking on the phone.

"Hey, Britt. Where's mom?" Beth asked.

Usually Brittany's response to being interrupted on the phone registered on the Richter scale, but today she put a hand over the mouthpiece and said, "At Mark Twain. She and Dad had a conference with Todd's teacher. It seems our saintly brother was involved in a mutiny over a substitute teacher."

Beth chuckled. She was dying to ask her sister more about the mutiny, but Brittany waved her off and went back to her conversation. There was no use asking Todd. He would blow the story up so big that she wouldn't be able to tell fact from fiction.

But why did he have to pick today for his mutiny? she wondered as she dumped her books on her bed. That was all her parents would want to talk about at dinner tonight. She wouldn't be able to get a word about the slumber party in edgewise.

"There isn't anything new about that," she grumbled out loud. Sometimes Brian's music was so loud that she had to talk out loud to hear her own thoughts above it. "SOMETIMES I EVEN HAVE TO YELL!" she shouted, knowing that no one would hear her.

It was always the same. Utter chaos. What's more, Alicia idolized Brittany and always bugged her and got into her makeup. Todd idolized Brian and always bugged him and got into his music. Brittany and Brian were always screaming at Alicia and Todd, who always screamed back, which made their parents constantly get after all four of them for fighting. Agatha loved the uproar, and she would run in circles barking. That left Beth to get attention the best way she could, and tonight—if Todd was in trouble at school—that wouldn't be easy. She would have to try hard.

Beth thought for a moment and then knelt beside her theater trunk, which stood in the corner near her closet. Actually the old steamer trunk had been a basement relic that she had rescued and cleaned up.

Now it was one of her most prized possessions, which, like vaudeville trunks in the olden days, was filled with the costumes and stage props she would use someday when she became an actress. But until then, when all else failed, she could always find the help she needed inside.

The *skre-e-ech* of the lid's being opened was lost in the twang of steel-string guitars coming from Brian's room next door. Beth rummaged around in the trunk, which smelled faintly of mildew, tossing out the gorilla costume Brian had worn one Halloween, an Oriental fan, wigs, fake mustaches and beards, and assorted pieces of clothing until, near the bottom, she found exactly what she was looking for.

She smiled as she pulled out a rectangular yellow box and read the words on the lid:

Wounds, Hurts, and Vampire Blood

A complete special-effects makeup lab

Use these specially designed professional quality makeups to create effects that look just like those you see in the movies.

This ought to get their attention, Beth thought gleefully. I'd like to see them ignore me now.

She opened the box and spread the contents out on her dresser. There were horrible-looking wounds made out of soft, flexible plastic, spirit-gum glue for sticking them onto skin, greasepaint makeup, including a purplish color for simulating bruises and black eyes, and skin tone for blending the artificial wounds into the person's skin color and making them look real. Last but not least was the tube marked VAMPIRE'S BLOOD. It would add the perfect touch.

For the next hour and a half Beth worked with the makeup kit, trying a nail wound here, a slash wound there, and bruises in first one place and then another. She was so absorbed that she barely heard when her parents got home, but she pricked up her ears when the doorbell rang a little later. She knew who that was: the kid who delivered pizza. That was normal on nights when her mother was running too late to cook supper.

"Come on kids! Time to eat!" she heard her father call from the bottom of the stairs.

Beth stepped in front of her mirror and smiled with satisfaction. Her dark hair was in total disarray, carefully teased to stick out in all the wrong places. Both eyes were bruised. A gash tore across her left cheek. Vampire blood trickled out of her nose.

"Perfect," she whispered as she pulled the tail of her blouse out of one side of her jeans. Racing to the door, she listened and waited.

There was the thunder of feet on the stairs fading away toward the kitchen and the scrape of chairs being pulled across the tile floor. Voices rose as her brothers and sisters scrambled over pizza slices and her father tried to bring order to the dinner table.

"Beth. You'd better come on," called her father. He was at the bottom of the stairs again. "The pizza's getting cold."

Beth opened her door just far enough to see the kitchen table and her father sitting down again. Everyone was munching contentedly and chattering, probably about Todd's latest fiasco. The moment for her grand entrance had arrived.

Opening her door, she grabbed for the railing, moaning pitifully as she limped down the stairs.

The kitchen got deathly still as all eyes fastened on her. Suddenly Agatha yipped, and her mother jumped to her feet.

"*E-LIZ-abeth!*" she shrieked.

CHAPTER

4

"So, what did your parents say?" Melanie eagerly asked the moment Beth got to school the next morning. "Do you get to have the slumber party?"

"No," mumbled Beth. "Not only that, I'm grounded."

"What!" shrieked Katie.

With a heavy sigh Beth explained the events of the evening before, ending with Mrs. Barry's reaction to the sight of her daughter's stumbling down the stairs.

"Don't you think you overdid it a little?" asked Christie.

"Yeah," agreed Jana. "She probably thought you'd been run over by a truck."

"Worse," Beth said grimly. "Anyway, I can't have

the slumber party, and I'm grounded for the entire weekend except for cheering at the football game Saturday afternoon. I can't even go to Bumpers afterward."

"Now what are we going to do?" Melanie asked in exasperation.

"You guys can go ahead and have a slumber party without me," offered Beth. She didn't want to admit how much she hated the thought of being left out of anything The Fabulous Five did. They had always done everything as a group, from going to modeling and charm school together, when Taffy Sinclair was trying to steal Melanie's friendship, to campaigning for Christie when she ran for president of the seventh grade. Still, Beth knew she had blown it with her parents this time. There was nothing else to do.

Jana gave her an understanding smile. "We can't do that," she said softly.

"You've certainly got that right," Katie said matter-of-factly. "There's no one left to come to our party. Laura has invited them all to hers."

"That's what I heard, too," said Christie. "I don't know how she's going to stuff so many kids into her bedroom."

"Apparently they're not going to stay in her bedroom very long," said Melanie. "Where do you think they're going to go after Mrs. Skinner goes to sleep and they sneak out of the house? Jana, can you find out from Funny Hawthorne?"

"No. Funny and I are friends, but she wouldn't give away any of Laura's secrets."

"Maybe they're going to Bumpers," suggested Christie.

"Or to a late movie," added Katie.

"Naw," said Beth. "That can't be it. Everyone is too excited. It has to be something really wild. Something spectacular."

Melanie's eyes got as round as saucers. "Maybe they're going to do something to us!"

"Forget it," said Katie. "Some of the girls going to Laura's party are our friends, too. They're just as excited as everyone else, and you know as well as I do that they wouldn't do anything mean to us."

"I guess you're right," admitted Melanie.

Beth looked down at the ground, making circles in the soft dirt with the toe of her sneaker and thinking hard about the situation. She had never felt so guilty in her life. Her friends were all being nice and not saying so, but it was her fault that they couldn't have a slumber party and talk some of the girls into coming to it instead of Laura's. That braggart, she thought as her anger swelled again. I'll fix her if it's the last thing I ever do.

"Listen, guys," she said hurriedly. "Don't tell anyone that our slumber party is canceled. Okay?"

"But what if somebody wants to come?" asked Christie.

"Right," said Katie. "What if someone says she

has thought it over and would rather be at our party than Laura's?"

"If that happens, tell them it's too late. Just say that what I'm planning for my slumber party is so terrific that only my very best friends—namely The Fabulous Five—are allowed to come now," she said with a grand sweep of her hand. "I'll explain later." She flashed her most theatrical smile and hurried away before anyone could insist that she explain now. She had just come up with a great idea, but she wanted to test it first before mentioning it to her friends.

The first seventh-grade girl she saw was Whitney Larkin. Whitney had gone to Copper Beach Elementary and was such a genius that she had skipped straight from fifth grade into seventh this year. Whitney made a lot of kids nervous because she was so smart, and they snickered at her behind her back and called her a baby. She was standing alone by the front gate. Probably watching for Curtis Trowbridge, thought Beth. He was a genius, too, and Whitney had seemed a lot happier since they had started dating. Beth didn't know her very well, but Whitney certainly seemed nice enough to her.

Beth slowed down so that she would not appear overly eager and walked toward Whitney.

"Hi, Whitney," she said as casually as she could.

Whitney looked around and smiled at Beth, murmuring hello.

Beth gave Whitney the most sympathetic look she could muster and said sadly, "I suppose you're going to Laura's party on Friday night."

Whitney's face brightened for an instant at the mention of the party and then crumpled into a frown. "What's the matter? Shouldn't I be?"

"Oh, of course you should," said Beth. "It's just a shame that so many of you got stuck having to go to Laura's party instead of mine. I guess I'll just have to start asking earlier next time. Still, I can't help thinking how much fun it would have been with you and Curtis there."

Whitney gasped. "Curtis?" she cried. "You're having *boys* at your slumber party?"

"Oh, they aren't going to stay all night," Beth assured her. "I'm just letting each girl ask a boy she likes for the early part of the evening. It's going to be so romantic. We'll probably sit up all night talking about it."

"Well . . . gee," fumbled Whitney. "Maybe I could tell Laura I can't come to her party and go to yours instead. I mean . . . if I could ask Curtis and everything."

"Oh, gosh, Whitney. I'm sorry," said Beth, looking deep into Whitney's eyes. "I really wish you could do that, but it's too late now. My parents decided that they had to know exactly how many would be there by last night. They're planning special food and stuff. You understand, don't you?"

Whitney nodded, and Beth could see that she was really disappointed. Her plan was working. Beth put a hand over her mouth and pretended to cough so that Whitney wouldn't notice the smile breaking over her face.

Next she sauntered up to Lisa Snow and Kim Baxter. After they exchanged greetings, she gave them the same sympathetic look she had given Whitney and said, "Gee. It's really too bad that you're going to Laura's party. I'm not trying to make you feel bad or anything, but I know you'd rather come to mine since you could have invited any boy you wanted."

Lisa and Kim looked stunned. "What are you talking about?" they asked together.

Beth put on her best wide-eyed-and-innocent look. "Didn't I tell you that you could invite boys when I asked you to my party yesterday?"

"No," snapped Kim. "All you said was that you were having a slumber party."

Beth braced herself for the outburst that she knew was coming. Again the two girls spoke in unison:

"Boys at a slumber party?"

Beth explained about how the boys would have to go home before bedtime and also that her parents had said she couldn't invite anyone else. Her excitement grew as she watched Lisa and Kim race off to spread the word about the terrific party they were missing, and she had to keep reminding herself that it wasn't really going to happen. It was only a harmless story she had made up to outdo Laura Mc-Call.

CHAPTER

5

"You told them WHAT?" shrieked Katie. Beth had motioned her four best friends to her locker when the first bell rang and everyone was getting their books. She had explained her plan, and Katie exploded. "There isn't even going to BE a slumber party, much less a party with BOYS!"

"Pipe down!" insisted Beth. "We have to outbrag Laura, don't we? Besides, how is anybody going to find out? They'll all be at Laura's. We could *pretend* to do anything we wanted to, and they'd never know the difference."

"Yeah . . . but . . ." fumbled Melanie.

"You should have seen the look on Lisa's and Kim's faces when I told them," Beth interrupted happily. "They were absolutely ILL. And Whitney Larkin, of all people, wanted to make up an excuse to back out on Laura's party and come to our party instead. Don't you see? Now we look like the big deals, and Laura and her friends look like the losers."

"It is sort of funny," admitted Jana. "Yesterday Laura had everybody all fired up to go to her party, and now, they all wish they were coming to ours."

By lunchtime it seemed to Beth that every girl in seventh grade wished she could be invited to Beth's nonexistent slumber party. Heather Clark and Melinda Thaler, seventh-graders from Riverfield, stopped Beth in the halls between classes to ask if what they had heard was true. The two girls had tried out for cheerleading along with Beth and Melanie, and Beth thought they looked more disappointed now because they couldn't come to her party than they had when they didn't make the squad.

Other girls had talked to her in classes during the day. Some of them were upset that they had been left out, and others were sorry that they were going to Laura's party instead of Beth's. But it was the reaction of Laura herself that made Beth the happiest at cheerleading practice after school.

"Does Laura know about our fake party yet?" Melanie asked when Beth trotted out to join her on the gym floor.

"I don't know," admitted Beth, "but I'd be awfully surprised if someone hasn't told her."

Just then Laura came breezing out of the dressing room with Tammy Lucero. Beth swallowed a giggle. Tammy was not only one of the members of Laura's exclusive clique, but in most people's opinion, she was the biggest gossip in the seventh grade. If anybody in The Fantastic Foursome had heard about Beth's boy-girl slumber party yet, it would be she.

Tammy was several inches shorter than Laura, and she had to skip to keep up with her tall friend's long strides. Beth watched in amusement as Tammy bounced along talking a mile a minute.

". . . and wait until I tell you what I just heard . . ." she was saying to Laura.

"Okay, girls. Attention, please," called Miss Wolfe, interrupting Tammy in midsentence. "Time to stop talking and start the *varm-ups*. Get into position for the leg-spread exercise."

Tammy tossed the German gym teacher a look of disgust and plopped down on the padded mat beside Laura. It was obvious to Beth that Tammy was bursting with news for her friend. It was also obvious that Tammy was avoiding looking in hers and Melanie's direction even though they were sitting opposite one another in a large circle on the floor. *She knows*, Beth thought, and she felt so terrific that she wanted to laugh out loud.

The girls spread their legs as far apart as possible, and Miss Wolfe led them in the exercise, counting out loud to ten as they touched chins to right knees and held the count. Next they touched chins to left knees for a ten count and then reached forward to rest their chins on the mat between their legs, and again, Miss Wolfe counted to ten. Beth hated this exercise. It was supposed to strengthen the muscles of the inner leg, and it hurt like crazy. But today she hardly felt a thing as she thought about how she was putting something big over on Laura McCall.

The girls remained on the floor for the leg squeeze and then, at Miss Wolfe's instruction, did five slow laps of the gym while Miss Wolfe hauled the floor mats to one side of the room. Beth watched out of the corner of her eye as Tammy and Laura lagged behind the others during laps. They're probably hoping that they can hang back and gossip while they're running without Miss Wolfe's seeing them, Beth mused. She stifled a laugh as the gym teacher called out to them to catch up with the others.

After the warm-ups the squad practiced cheers for the rest of the session, and there was still no talking allowed. Beth kept an eye on Tammy and Laura, and Melanie nudged her a couple of times between cheers when it looked as if Tammy might get her chance to tell Laura about the party, but each time Miss Wolfe interrupted with new instructions.

"For our final cheer today," Miss Wolfe said at last in her thick German accent, "ve vill do 'Electrify.'"

It was a favorite with most of the squad—short, snappy, and ending in a jump—and the girls began to applaud. Miss Wolfe held up her hand to signify that she had not finished talking, but out of the corner of her eye Beth could see that Tammy and Laura were having a conversation of their own and were not listening to Miss Wolfe.

"Ve vill make one change from the vay ve usually do this cheer. Instead of finishing vith a spread eagle, I vant you to end the cheer vith a herkie. Now line up, please."

"Wow," Beth muttered under her breath. The spread eagle was the easiest cheerleading jump, but the herkie was definitely the most difficult. While the left leg and arm are out to the side in half of an airborne split, the right leg is bent at the knee and the right arm is straight up in the air. Beth had only done the herkie correctly two or three times in cheerleading practice, while Laura McCall was practically an expert.

Beth glanced quickly at Tammy and Laura while the squad was lining up. They were at the far end of the line from Miss Wolfe, and Tammy was keeping one eye on the teacher while she talked rapidly into Laura's ear. At first Beth was disappointed that Laura's expression was blank, but then she began to notice a change, the eyes enlarging and the chest swelling as if something was boiling up inside the tall, blond girl and was about to erupt. Beth didn't have time to react because head cheerleader Dekeisha Adams was starting the cheer.

Gonna raise our spirits
Up up high
Gonna raise our spirits
ELECTRIFY!

On the last word of the cheer the squad vaulted into the air, all, that is, except for Laura McCall. "What!" she shrieked, turning an angry, red face toward Beth.

Beth knew that Miss Wolfe didn't notice how poorly she executed her herkie or that Taffy Sinclair and Dekeisha almost bumped into each other in midair or even that Tammy had done the spread eagle instead of the herkie. She couldn't have. She was glaring straight at Laura.

"Laura McCall, for that outburst and for failing even to attempt the jump, you vill stay late and do ten perfect herkies," she commanded. "The rest of the squad is dismissed."

Beth grabbed Melanie's arm and rocketed out of the gym. She didn't even bother to look back at Laura, who stood alone in the center of the gym floor. Who needs to? Beth reasoned. My plan is working. Laura's the one who looks foolish now, and I'm the one who's winning!

CHAPTER

6

*F*riday evening was always a bigger zoo than usual at the Barry house, and this Friday evening was no exception. Beth marched into the family room after supper in the middle of an argument between Brian and Brittany, who were each trying to persuade their father that it was their turn to take the van. "You had it last night," argued Brian.

Brittany raised her eyebrows. "So I had to go to the library. That doesn't count."

"It does so," insisted Brian. "Dad, she can't have it two nights in a row. It's not fair."

"Oh, NO?" Brittany protested. "Who had it both Friday and Saturday nights last weekend? Huh? Tell me that!"

"Not me!" Beth interjected brightly. "I never have

it. Which means that I ought to at least get to have a friend over tonight."

Brittany threw her a drop-dead look. "I thought you were grounded."

"So-o-o-o? My friends aren't."

"Bug off, Beth," Brian demanded. "This is important."

"Oh, yeah?" Beth pushed her face up close to Brian's. "Since when did you get to be such a big deal?" Then turning to her father, she said, "So can I have a friend over? *Please.*"

Before he could answer, Mrs. Barry came into the room. Alicia and Todd hurried after her, each waving a VCR tape. Agatha bounded after all of them, jumping for the waving tapes as if they were treats.

"I've got to watch *Conan The Destroyer* first!" shouted Todd, pushing Agatha aside.

"*Lady and the Tramp! Lady and the Tramp!*" chanted Alicia. "I HATE *Conan The Destroyer.* And Agafa, you get down!"

I might as well forget about getting a chance to ask anything, Beth thought, sighing with resignation and burrowing her face into Agatha's furry black-and-white head. It was always the same. Everyone got attention but her. Besides, she reasoned, I'm grounded and they wouldn't let me have one of my friends over anyway. It's useless to ask.

Dragging Agatha with her, she drifted upstairs and into her room feeling like the loneliest person on earth. The kitchen clock had said a quarter of seven a few minutes ago when she left that room to look for her father in the family room. That meant girls were beginning to arrive at Laura's apartment now for the big slumber party. She didn't even have to close her eyes to picture the scene. She could see it all.

Laura would be standing at the door looking cool and in control, as usual. Girls would be pouring in, tossing their sleeping bags wherever they could find floor space and giggling in anticipation of a terrific time with *no parents* around to keep an eye on them. The other members of The Fantastic Foursome— Laura's slaves, thought Beth—would probably be serving refreshments while Laura flicked her long blond braid and sent Mrs. Skinner to her room.

"Close the door and don't come out until morning," Beth could almost hear Laura call after her.

"Poor Mrs. Skinner," Beth said aloud to Agatha. "I know just how she feels."

By eight-thirty the Barry house had quieted down. The front door had slammed twice. Just after it slammed the first time a car started up in the driveway. The second time it slammed, a boy's voice called out, "Come on, Brian, jump in." All of this told Beth that Brittany had won out in the battle over the van, and Brian had been left to call a friend for a ride.

Beth's thoughts went back to Laura's party for the

millionth time. "What do you suppose they're doing now, Agatha?"

The dog twisted her head from side to side as if she were trying to understand.

"Probably having a super time. Gorging themselves with food. And smoking. Girls always smoke at slumber parties," she assured Agatha, who lowered herself onto the floor with a bored sigh.

Beth sighed, too. It wouldn't be long until nine o'clock. Had everybody sneaked out of Laura's apartment by now to do whatever big deal thing it was that she had planned?

"It's probably nothing," Beth scoffed. "Laura just likes to brag and make people think that she has it made."

Feeling restless, she opened her closet door. A full-length mirror hung on the inside. I could practice cheers, she thought. Miss Wolfe had told them that ninety percent of their practice time away from the gym should be spent in front of a mirror. She claimed it helped to get good definition of movement, which meant that your arms and legs were straight and moving in perfect time with the beat. Beth sighed. She was restless, it was true, but she didn't really feel like working on good definition of movement, no matter how important it was. Not tonight. Not with everyone but her and her friends at Laura McCall's party.

Just then the doorbell rang. Beth jumped in surprise, and Agatha ran to the window, put her front paws on the sill, and barked like crazy at whoever was below at the door.

"Beth! You have company," her father shouted from below.

My friends! she thought. I knew they wouldn't desert me.

She raced down the stairs with Agatha right behind her, feeling glad that she hadn't pressed her father to let someone come over. He would probably have said no anyway, she reasoned. But now, with her friends here on their own, surely he wouldn't make them leave.

Mr. Barry was in the foyer frowning as she approached, and he reached out and grabbed Agatha by the collar. Beth wondered for a split second why he did that. The big sheepdog loved all of The Fabulous Five. She only growled at strangers. Then Beth threw the door open wide and froze to the spot.

The front lawn was covered with seventh-grade girls, and on the doorstep stood Laura McCall.

CHAPTER

7

*B*eth could just barely hear Agatha growling over the pounding of her heart. She prayed she would faint, or die, or anything that would keep her from having to stand there in front of Laura McCall one second longer.

Laura stood with her hands behind her back and smiled slyly. "So, where's the big party you're supposed to be having tonight?" she asked loudly so everyone could hear.

Beth cringed. In the darkness beyond the glow of the porch light she could make out lots of familar faces waiting for her answer. Dekeisha Adams and Mandy McDermott were on the sidewalk leading up to the front door. Alexis Duvall and Kim Baxter stood beside the oak tree with some girls from Cop-

41

per Beach. Even Whitney Larkin was peering at her from the shadows.

Giggles rippled through the crowd on the lawn.

Beth reached behind and closed the front door so that her father wouldn't be able to hear. Her mind was racing. She couldn't let Laura McCall make an idiot of her in front of all these girls.

"Everybody's downstairs . . . in the basement playroom," she stammered. "I'd invite you in, but it's already too crowded."

"The boys are there, too?" Laura asked innocently.

"Sure," answered Beth. She was feeling more confident by the moment. Laura wasn't going to make a fool out of her. Everybody believed that she had invited boys to her party, and she was going to make sure they kept right on believing it. "They're having a blast. Too bad you couldn't think up something as great as inviting boys to your party. Then you wouldn't have to go out looking for a good time."

Laura chuckled. "Oh, we've already had a good time. But tell me more about the boys. What are they doing right now?"

Red warning lights flashed in Beth's mind. Laura was up to something. But what? The crowd of girls was slowly drawing in closer, and the rest of The Fantastic Foursome had gathered around Laura.

Now she could see Gloria Drexler and Marcie Bee moving forward too.

"Since I can't see them *right now,* I couldn't tell you exactly what they are doing, could I?" she answered nervously.

"So, what do you *think* they're doing?" prodded Laura.

"Eating, maybe," offered Beth. "Or dancing. That's what they're probably doing right now. Dancing with the girls."

"Or maybe they're at home," challenged Laura. "At home watching television like Keith Masterson is doing at this very moment."

Beth gasped, feeling as if she were part of an old vaudeville act and had just gotten a pie in the face.

Laura's eyes were gleaming as she went on. "We just came from Keith's house, and he acted as if he had been home all evening."

"So did Randy Kirwan," added Melissa McConnell.

"And Tony Calcaterra and all of the other guys," said Tammy Lucero.

"You haven't been to Keith's house," Beth shouted angrily. "Or any of the others' houses, for that matter."

"Oh, yes, we have," shouted Funny Hawthorne. "We've been out TPing cute guys' houses ever since it got dark. Wheee!" she squealed, and pulled a roll of toilet paper from behind her back and tossed it toward the tree that grew by Beth's front door. "And we've saved our leftover toilet paper for *your* house!"

As if on cue, toilet paper streamers filled the sky, falling over bushes and trees, and almost empty rolls landed with a *thunk!* on a dozen spots on the roof. Beth ducked as one of the rolls slid down the peak and bounced off her head.

Girls were running back and forth across the lawn, laughing wildly and spreading toilet paper over everything until the Barry front yard looked as if it had been hit by a pastel blizzard. Only Laura didn't join in. She stood to one side of the front steps, arms folded over her chest, and watched, wearing a satisfied expression.

So that was what Laura had dreamed up for her party that had everyone so excited, Beth mused. TPing cute boys' houses! And that was also how she had been able to find out that Beth hadn't invited Keith and the others to a big party. Still, she reasoned, she had never said which boys were invited. For all Laura knew, she might have invited eighth-graders or boys from another school. And if Laura really had mentioned her party to Keith, well . . . She had until the football game tomorrow to figure out what to tell Keith.

Inside her own house Beth could hear Agatha going crazy, barking and throwing herself against the front door. That made her remember her parents. What were they doing? Even worse, what were they thinking?

She didn't have to wonder long, because suddenly the door opened and her father stepped out. "Hey! What's going on out here?"

"Oh . . . well, just . . . a few of my friends . . . " Beth sputtered, ". . . having some fun."

Crinkles appeared around Mr. Barry's eyes, and his face lit up. "TPing, eh? We used to do that when I was a kid. Looks like you'll have the job of cleaning it up, though," he added with a laugh. "They're your friends."

Just then another roll slid off the roof and bounced on his head. He looked startled for an instant, then said as he backed through the door, "Yup. We used to do a lot of TPing when I was a kid."

When he had gone inside, Beth nearly collapsed from relief. Not only had her father not been angry, but most of the girls had disappeared as soon as he came out of the house. The rest were scurrying away now. Even Laura was gone. Thank goodness, Beth thought. If she had said one more thing about the boys, I would have absolutely *died*.

Agatha greeted her excitedly when she went back into the house, jumping up and licking her face as if she had been gone for ages. She was still wrestling with Agatha when Alicia tugged at her shirt.

"There you are, Beth Barry!" Alicia scolded, as if she had been searching all over for her sister. "The phone's for you. You'd better hurry. It's Keith, and he sure sounds mad."

CHAPTER

8

"I thought you were grounded," Keith grumbled as soon as Beth picked up the phone and said hello.

"I am grounded," she insisted. "For the whole weekend."

"Oh, yeah? Then what about the slumber party Laura McCall says you're having? The one with boys?"

Beth fought down a wave of panic. She had hoped Keith wouldn't hear about that. But she hadn't counted on Laura McCall's TPing his house, either. Laura had said they saw Keith and the other boys, but she didn't say anything about talking to them or mentioning Beth's party. She would have to think fast, but as she struggled to answer him, her lips felt stiff, and the words came out slowly.

"Laura was just making that up." Do I sound convincing? Beth thought wildly. Or can he tell I'm the one making things up? "You know how she feels about The Fabulous Five," she went on urgently. "She'd say anything to make us look bad."

"I don't know," Keith mumbled. "She wasn't the only one talking about your party. Some of the other girls were, too. Whitney Larkin even said that you told her that if she came to your party, she could invite Curtis."

"If you don't believe me, call my friends," Beth challenged. "Call Jana or Christie or Katie or Melanie. They're probably at home, and they'll tell you that I'm not having a slumber party, much less inviting boys to it. How could I, when I'm grounded? Besides!" she went on breathlessly. "If you really liked me, you'd *trust* me!"

"Okay. Okay," said Keith. He still sounded a little miffed, but Beth breathed a small sigh of relief as he said, "I just wondered why I wasn't invited if it was true."

"Of course I'd invite you," Beth assured him. "I wish I could have a party and invite boys, but I doubt if my parents would let me. Whenever I mention it, my dad always says that things are crazy enough around here without any *more* kids."

Keith laughed at that, and they talked for a little while longer. After they hung up, Beth sprawled across her bed. She could hear Agatha whimpering outside her door, but she had too much on her mind to get up and let her in.

Life had been so simple back at Mark Twain Elementary when she and her friends had only Taffy Sinclair to deal with instead of Laura McCall and the rest of The Fantastic Foursome.

What was she going to do now that Laura had called her bluff on the fake slumber party? Laura had not only had a real slumber party with everyone getting to TP cute boys' houses, but she had caught Beth in a lie.

And what was worse, Keith had been really mad when he thought she was having a party and hadn't invited him. She had liked Keith for ages, and he had been her boyfriend ever since they went to a movie together with a big gang of sixth-graders last year. Since then they had gone out several times and always met at Bumpers after football games.

There was no doubt about it, Laura was out to get her and her friends, and so far Laura was ahead. In fact, it was Laura McCall: 2, Beth Barry: 0.

She heard the faint ring of the phone through her closed door, and a moment later Todd called out, "Beth! Phone!"

It's probably Laura calling to rub it in, she thought as she scuffed down the hall.

"Hello," she said, and crossed her fingers behind her back for luck.

"Beth Barry, how could you do such a thing?"

It was Jana, and she sounded positively furious.

"What are you talking about?" Beth asked in surprise.

"You know what I'm talking about," said Jana. "Your dumb idea of bragging to everybody that you were going to have a slumber party tonight and invite boys. Randy just called. He said he heard about it from the girls who TPed his house."

"Well, he obviously didn't believe it," said Beth. "Otherwise he wouldn't have called you because he wouldn't have thought you were at home."

"He called your house first," said Jana. "But your line was busy. So then he called here. He was so mad that if I hadn't been home, he would probably have broken up with me, and it would be all your fault."

"Come on, Jana," pleaded Beth. "You know I didn't mean for anything like that to happen. I was just trying to get back at Laura for making The Fabulous Five look like a bunch of losers."

"Well, if you ask me, it backfired."

Jana slammed down the phone in Beth's ear, but now it was Beth's turn to be angry. How could Jana blame me? How could she possibly think it was my fault that Laura McCall was making fools out of us? she thought desperately. How could anybody think that? It wasn't fair.

Beth stomped back to her room, grabbed the pillow off her bed, and hurled it into the floor. Her life had turned into a roller coaster ride: up one minute and in the pits the next—and it was all because of Laura. She would get her for this if it was the last thing she ever did.

"Watch out, Laura McCall," she muttered under her breath. "From now on, it's all-out war."

CHAPTER

9

*B*eth had intended to spend the whole weekend figuring out a way to get back at Laura McCall, but that was before she glanced into the mirror Saturday morning and made a horrible discovery. A pimple, huge, red, and ugly, was beaming out like a beacon in the night from just left of her nose.

"What!" she gasped. "Where did *that* thing come from?"

It hadn't been there last night. She had washed her face before she went to bed, and there was definitely no sign then of Mount Everest erupting on her face for all the world to see. How could she possibly go down to breakfast looking like this?

Beth could already hear her father in the kitchen, singing at the top of his lungs and going through his

regular Saturday-morning pancake ritual. Her father made the best pancakes in the world—or so *he*
said—and every Saturday morning the whole family
gathered at the breakfast table together to sample his
latest concoctions. It was a tradition in the Barry
family and practically the only time during their
busy week when they could all eat together. She
would get killed if she didn't show up within the
next fifteen minutes.

She glanced at herself in the mirror again, and
tears shot into her eyes. *But I can't go down there looking like this!* she thought desperately.

Beth rummaged through the jumble of aspirins
and ointments and other odds and ends in the medi-
cine cabinet looking for the Band-Aids and praying
that the box wouldn't be empty. Alicia was crazy
about Band-Aids. Whenever anyone else in the family had a Band-Aid, she always wanted one for herself, and it had to go onto the exact same spot. That
meant that half the time the Band-Aid box was
empty. She shook it, hearing a faint rustling sound,
and opened it to find one lonely Band-Aid inside.

Grabbing it, she stuck it over the pimple just as
Todd banged on the bathroom door and yelled,
"Come on. Breakfast is ready."

For once in her life Beth was glad that no one in
her family ever noticed her as she slunk down the
stairs and slid into her place at the table. Leaning on
her elbow, she slumped over her plate and covered

the left side of her face with her hand. All she had to do was stay in that position until she had finished her pancakes, and she would be home free.

"Cut yourself shaving?" Brian asked offhandedly from across the table.

Beth froze. Whom was he talking to?

"Hey, Beth. I asked you a question," he said, and this time she could hear laughter in his voice. "Did you cut yourself shaving? Hey, everybody. Beth's started shaving!"

He broke out laughing for real this time, and she could feel all eyes turn on her.

"Bethy! Bethy!" Alicia shrieked. "Why are you shaving? You're a *girl*!"

"I'm not shaving," Beth mumbled, still staring down at the soggy lumps of pancakes swimming in syrup in her plate. "Now leave me alone, Brian."

"Sure she's shaving," Brian insisted. "Why else would she have a Band-Aid on her face?"

Mrs. Barry leaned toward Beth, probably to inquire if she was feeling okay. But before anybody else could say anything Brittany intervened.

"Knock it off, Brian. She probably just found her first zit. Believe me, I know how it feels. Of course, you wouldn't. Your whole head's a zit! You're the only one I know who looks *better* covered with pimples."

"Children!" Mrs. Barry warned just as Beth was groaning and wishing she could become invisible.

Why was this happening? Why couldn't they all just shut up? What a miserable time to be noticed.

"Oh, my gosh!" Brian shouted, completely ignoring his mother. "Her first zit? Look out, everybody! Another teenager has just been unleashed on the world." He cupped his hands around his mouth and appeared to be shouting to someone outside the back door. "Look out, world! Here comes another case of adolescent behavior to drive you nuts."

"Mom! Dad! Can't you do something about this moron?" Beth shouted, jumping to her feet and pulling her hand away from her face so quickly that she accidentally ripped off her Band-Aid, exposing the huge red pimple that pulsed with flaming heat. That was absolutely the last straw, and she spun and raced back up the stairs to hide in her room.

Belly-flopping so hard onto her bed that she bounced, Beth buried her face in her pillow. Zits! Adolescent behavior! Baloney! How dare Brian make fun of her. And how dare Britanny say she knew how it felt. Brittany didn't know how anything felt. Not anything that I feel, anyway, she thought.

Beth was still lying on her bed staring into space a little while later when there was a soft knock on her door.

"Who is it?" she growled.

"Mom."

Beth sighed. "Come in," she said, but she made

sure that her voice sounded as put out as she felt. The last thing she needed was a lecture from her mother.

"Hi, honey," said Mrs. Barry as she came into the room. "I'm sorry there was such a scene at the breakfast table, but you know how this family is. Are you feeling better now?"

"Yeah," Beth lied.

"That's good," Mrs. Barry said, bending close to look at the left side of Beth's face. "I'm on my way to the grocery store now so I'll pick up something for your face while I'm there. With any luck, it will practically be gone by time for school Monday."

School. Beth's eyes widened. She had totally forgotten about school. She nodded mutely to her mother and was just about to go into a fit of panic over how she was going to face the kids at school with the world's largest zit when her mother popped back in the door and said, "I almost forgot. Dad said to remind you to get out in the front yard and clean all the toilet paper off the trees and bushes. He wants it done today."

Great, she thought. That's just great! It's not enough that I have the world's largest pimple; now I have to expose it to the world.

CHAPTER

10

A chilly wind was blowing toilet paper into the neighboring yards by the time Beth got outside. She had armed herself with a leaf rake and a couple of black plastic trash bags, and she went right to work cleaning the paper off the grass and snagging it out of the trees and off the bushes, desperately hoping that she could get the job completed before anyone could come down her street and see her—and her *enormous* zit.

"Bethy! Bethy! Don't throw that away," Alicia shouted, racing out the door and down the front steps. "I need that for Nibbles."

Puzzled, Beth glanced down at the empty toilet paper tube she had been about to throw into the trash bag. Nibbles was Alicia's hamster, who had gotten his name when he ate his way out of his cardboard carton on the way home from the pet shop. "What does Nibbles want with this?" she asked.

"I'm making a laboratory for him," Alicia said proudly.

Beth chuckled. "A laboratory? What's he going to do in a laboratory? Discover a cure for cancer?"

Alicia put her hands on her hips and looked up at her older sister in complete exasperation. "No. He's going to run through it and play hide-and-seek."

"Oh," Beth said. "You mean a labyrinth."

Alicia cocked her head to one side and frowned. "That's what I said. A LAB-ratory."

"All right. All right," said Beth. "I get it. You want me to save these for you. Is that it?"

Alicia nodded. "Mom's driving me to my ballet lesson now, so don't throw any away. Okay?"

Beth shrugged and turned back to her task. It would go slower now that she had to separate out the empty tubes from the paper. It was no wonder. Hadn't Funny Hawthorne said that they had saved the last of their toilet paper rolls for her house? That meant there were at least a million tubes. It would take her all day to clean up the mess.

To make matters worse, her pimple was throbbing. "Nobody ever told me that these things hurt," she grumbled as she hauled the first full trash bag around to the driveway. When her mother had returned from the grocery store a little while earlier, she had handed Beth a tube of ointment that Beth had dabbed carefully on the angry spot. That had been at least half an hour ago, and so far, it wasn't doing the least bit of good.

She was just starting to come around the corner of the house and into the front yard again when she heard the screech of rusty bicycle brakes. *Keith!* she thought in a panic. She would know the sound of his brakes anywhere.

It was too late to duck back along the side of the house. He had already seen her and was waving and grinning like crazy.

"Hey, Beth," he called as he parked his bike and stooped to scoop up a handful of toilet paper off the grass. "It looks as if they got you, too. I just finished cleaning my yard. Want some help?"

Beth tried to smile, but it made her pimple hurt more than ever. He was coming toward her. Any minute now he would be close enough to see her terrible zit. Her knees were getting weak. What am I going to do? she begged silently.

Makeup! The word floated down from heaven like an answer to a prayer.

"Wait here," she shouted, backing toward the front door. "I'll get us some hot chocolate. I'm freezing. Aren't you?"

She barely heard Keith call out, "Can't I come in while you're fixing it?" as she bumped up the concrete steps and stumbled in the door.

She couldn't help it if Keith thought she was weird for not inviting him in the way she always did. She would think up an excuse when she went back outside. Right now, she had an important mission: to sneak into Brittany's room and get some makeup to cover her zit.

"If only Alicia were here," she muttered under her breath as she raced up the stairs. Alicia was a genius when it came to sneaking into Brittany's room, and she knew exactly where their older sister kept all of her makeup, too. Oh, well, she thought. I'll just have to do it myself. At least Agatha hadn't heard her come into the house and bounded along to crash into things and get in the way. One thing's going her way was better than nothing's.

Stopping in the upstairs hall, Beth surveyed the scene. Brittany's bedroom door was slightly ajar, and the shower was going in the bathroom. Brittany was right on schedule. Thank goodness she was predictable, Beth thought. Her sister had the same routine every Saturday. Go down for pancake breakfast with the family. Talk on the phone. Take a shower. Talk on the phone. Blow dry and curl her hair. Talk on the phone. Get dressed and *finally* go out to meet her friends.

Beth took a deep breath and pushed Brittany's door open. Stepping inside, she kept one ear tuned to the sound of the shower as she frantically searched for signs of her sister's makeup. She grabbed Britt's purse and began jumbling around inside. Wallet. Breath mints. Lipstick. Hairbrush. Period. That was it. Beth tossed the purse aside and began pulling out drawers from the bureau. She must have stashed it in here, she thought.

She was poking around in the third drawer from the bottom when she stood up straight and listened. The shower had stopped.

"Oh, my gosh," she whispered. When did that happen? Brittany could be on her way back to her room right this instant.

Beth didn't bother to close the drawer or even look up and down the hall as she zipped out of Brittany's room and into her own, collapsing onto the floor. She would kill me if she caught me in her room, Beth thought when her heart quieted down enough for her to hear her own thoughts. She'd murder me. Only Alicia could get away with a thing such as that.

A second later she remembered what this was all about in the first place. *Keith*. He was outside waiting for her to bring hot chocolate. Beth crawled to her window, pulled herself up onto her knees, and peeked out. His bike was still in the driveway. She had been afraid for a moment that he might have gotten tired of waiting and gone home. Half of her wished he had. She still had the awful zit, and borrowing Brittany's makeup had just become an impossible dream.

Beth sat down on the floor and rested the back of her head on the sill. She couldn't go downstairs to talk to Keith looking like *this*. The Band-Aid box was empty. She had used the last one herself. If only she had asked her mother to pick up another box at the grocery store.

Just then her gaze fell on her theater trunk, and an idea began to form in her mind.

"Why not?" she asked out loud. "It worked on my parents—sort of."

Throwing open the trunk lid, she rummaged through the contents until she found the rectangular yellow box with the words on top that said:

Wounds, Hurts, and Vampire Blood

Smiling slyly to herself, Beth opened the box and went to work.

"What took you so long?" Keith asked as Beth scooted out the door carrying two cups of hot chocolate a few minutes later. Then suddenly his eyes seemed to focus on her face and he went pale. "What happened to you?" he shrieked.

It took every bit of acting talent that Beth possessed to keep from breaking up, but she managed to hold a straight face. She had wanted to cover her pimple with a gross-looking puncture wound but decided that would be carrying things a bit too far. Instead she had settled for a pair of bruises made by combining red and blue greasepaint into a horrible purplish color. One bruise covered the zit on the left side of her nose, and the other decorated her forehead. Now she walked toward Keith, trying her best to look a little weak and fluttery.

"Oh, nothing," she said. "I was just playing with Agatha, and she accidentally knocked me into the wall."

"Gosh, that's too bad," he said, and Beth almost died from relief. "I'll bet that really hurt."

Together they had the yard cleaned up in record time and collected a huge pile of toilet paper tubes for Alicia. Keith laughed when Beth told him about Alicia's "laboratory" for Nibbles.

"Wow!" said Keith, staring at his watch. "I didn't realize it was so late. I've got to get to the stadium and get ready for the game." Then he looked at her with a worried expression and asked, "Are you going to be able to cheer today with those bruises on your face?"

Beth was stunned. She tried to nod as Keith jumped on his bike and gave her one last wave before he rode away, but all she could concentrate on was how she had been in such a panic to cover up her pimple that she had forgotten all about cheering at the game today. Now what was she going to do?

Missing a game without a life-or-death excuse meant getting kicked off the squad. At the same time, she couldn't possibly show up looking like this, and if she washed off the fake bruises, Keith would suspect that she was lying again.

CHAPTER

11

*B*eth was staring at her fake bruises in the bathroom mirror and wondering what on earth she was going to do when she heard a horn honk in the driveway. A split second later Brittany's bedroom door slammed and she clattered down the stairs, making more noise than a stampede of elephants.

The house was totally quiet now. Brian was at his Saturday job bagging groceries at a supermarket; Mom had taken Alicia to her ballet lesson; Todd had gone to a friend's house; her dad was in the garage refinishing an old chair; and even Agatha had gone off somewhere to nap. It was the perfect chance to go back into Brittany's bedroom and use some of her makeup. This time she didn't even have to sneak.

When she left for the football stadium a little

while later, she was ecstatic. "Not only am I a terrific actress," she told herself as she walked along, "I'm also a super makeup artist."

Her first impulse had been to wash off the bruises and just use the makeup to hide her pimple. But that could get her into trouble with Keith, she had reminded herself. Instead she decided to apply Brittany's flesh-toned foundation, called Shimmering Gloss, right on top of the fake bruises. That way, if Keith asked any questions, she could always rub off just a little bit of the foundation and show him that the bruises were still underneath. Best of all, buried beneath layers of gooey stage makeup and Shimmering Gloss was the horrid pimple. No one would ever know it was there.

Melanie was waiting for her outside the main gate of the stadium. She was easy to spot in the milling crowd because she was wearing her short, cardinal-red cheerleading skirt and gold letter sweater, just as Beth was, and she bounced on her tiptoes and waved to Beth with a red-and-gold pom-pon.

"Hi," Melanie said brightly, and if she noticed Beth's makeup, she didn't let on. Instead her eyes got big and she began talking excitedly. "Boy, have I got a lot of stuff to tell you. Alexis just told me all about Laura's slumber party last night, and wait until you hear what happened."

"I already know what happened," grumbled Beth.

"They went out TPing cute boys' houses and then came to mine. They also know that I didn't have a slumber party last night and invite boys."

"Yeah," said Melanie. "Alexis told me all about that, but that's not everything. She said just a minute ago that Laura said she might make her clique bigger and let some more kids in. She was even making up new names, like The Sensational Seven, The Exotic Eight, and . . . get this," Melanie added with a tinkling laugh, *The Naughty Nine*. Alexis said that girls were making idiots of themselves trying to do things for Laura and get on her good side. Everybody wants to be in her group. And you'll never guess who some of them are."

Melanie didn't give Beth a chance to answer. "Kim Baxter and Sara Sawyer and Lisa Snow! Our old friends from Mark Twain Elementary, of all people. Alexis said she didn't want in Laura's clique, but I'm not so sure. All she could talk about was Laura McCall and the things her dad lets her get away with."

"Big deal!" Beth said with a sniff. It made her furious to think of their old friends buttering up Laura McCall. "So what if Laura can get away with things? That doesn't mean her friends can get away with them."

"Oh, yes, it does," argued Melanie. "All they have to do is hang around with her. They just tell their parents that they're going over to her apartment. Then when Laura does something, they do it, too. None of their parents ever finds out."

Beth was just about to explode and yell at Melanie that if she was that impressed with what Laura's friends could do, then why didn't she try to get into the clique, too, when Whitney Larkin and Mandy McDermott stormed up to her.

"What's the big idea, Beth Barry?" demanded Whitney. "Were you trying to make us look stupid, or something?"

"Yeah," said Mandy. "You said *you* were having a slumber party and inviting *boys*. But when we came to your house last night to TP, there wasn't a single boy there, or girls either, for that matter. What if we had skipped Laura's party thinking we were going to yours? We would have been the laughingstock of Wacko Junior High when everybody found out."

"Just like *you* are now!" added Whitney. "And it serves you right."

The two girls whirled around and marched toward the stadium gate with their noses in the air.

Beth watched them go in stunned silence. Then she turned to Melanie. "I told them it was too late for them to be included in my party," she argued. "I didn't want them to think that they were really invited—just that our party was going to be better than Laura's. What do they mean, I'm the laughingstock of Wacko Junior High?"

"Eeek!" squeaked Melanie. "That was the other thing I wanted to tell you, but I didn't know how."

"Well, you'd better tell me right now," warned Beth.

"Okay. Here goes," Melanie said with a sigh. "I hate to say this because we're good friends, but you're starting to get a terrible reputation. Everybody says that you have a super extralarge mouth and that nobody can believe a word you say. They say that you make up things just to get noticed. They say that they're tired of it and that your big story about the slumber party was absolutely the last straw."

"Who says that?" Beth demanded.

Melanie looked down at her shoes. "Practically everybody," she murmured.

Beth stared at her friend without moving a muscle or blinking an eye, but inside she felt as if she were crumpling into a tiny ball and growing smaller and smaller by the second. How could Melanie say such a thing? she wondered. How could *anybody* say such a thing? It was incredible. They just didn't understand her. That was all.

"Well, I'll show them," she muttered under her breath. "I'll show every single one of them. And I'll do it by making them see the truth about Laura McCall."

CHAPTER

12

*B*eth couldn't ignore the angry looks she got when she and Melanie joined some of the other cheerleaders on the sidelines beside the Wakeman Warriors' bench where they were waiting for the team to come out of the locker room. Taffy Sinclair and Alexis Duvall were there, and they started whispering as soon as she got near. She glanced at the cheering section up in the stands. It was almost filled, and all the kids there seemed to be talking among themselves. Gossiping, she thought. And she was sure the gossip was all about her.

Just then Laura and Tammy came bounding up, grinning as if they were bursting with news.

"Guess what, everybody," Laura called as the

other members of the squad gathered around her. "Have I ever got some terrific news."

Beth hung back, staying just far enough to be out of the crowd around Laura but close enough to hear what she was saying. The others were pushing to get nearer to her, including Melanie, Beth noticed, and frowned.

"Everybody knows that Brain Damage is going to do a concert here next Friday night, right?" Laura nodded to the girls, and almost everyone nodded back.

Beth didn't respond, but she definitely knew that the wacky English rock band was coming to town. They were the craziest bunch of teen musicians on the planet, dressing in outlandish costumes and sometimes even dragging kids out of the audience to join their group for a song or two. It was always big news when they scheduled a concert. In fact, it had been plastered all over the newspaper for weeks, and everyone was going. But what did that have to do with Laura? Beth wondered.

"Well, get this," Laura went on, flicking the end of her long blond braid and giving Beth a look of superiority. "My father is a personal friend of the promoter who is handling Brain Damage's North American tour, but that's not all. Daddy said that he can get front row seats for me and any of my friends!"

Beth could feel the blood draining out of her face as a wild whoop went up from the cheerleading squad. Everybody—except for Beth and Melanie—was jumping around and hugging each other and squealing about how cute the rock stars were.

"Front row tickets to Brain Damage!" Dekeisha shrieked. "I think I'm going to die!"

Most of the others scrambled toward the cheering section to tell their friends, and Beth watched in disgust as word spread through the crowd like a wave. How could this be happening to me *now?* she thought. Just when I absolutely have to get even with Laura, she's going to get front row tickets to Brain Damage! It was almost more than Beth could stand, and when she looked Laura's way, she saw every conceivable shade of purple and red.

A moment later the Wakeman Warriors jogged onto the field to the roar of the crowd and began their warm-up calisthenics. Beth caught sight of Keith in the second row. He was smiling at her, and she waved a pom-pon back in his direction. Suddenly she remembered her pimple, safely hidden under layers of goop. Thank goodness, she thought, breathing a huge sigh of relief. A fiery pimple blazing beside her nose would have made her day even more unbearable than it already was.

Dekeisha signaled the squad onto the field, and Beth tried to concentrate on the cheers. She was going through all the motions and saying all the words, but she could tell that she wasn't at her best. Her definition of movement was lousy, and each time she did a jump, she came back to earth like a ton of bricks. She looked at Laura out of the corner of her eye and scowled. It was all Laura's fault. Laura's fault that Beth had had to make up a story about a slumber party. Laura's fault that she was getting the reputation of having a super extralarge mouth. Laura's fault about *everything*!

Beth was beginning to perspire. The chilly wind that had been blowing this morning had died away, and her gold letter sweater was beginning to itch. To make matters worse, Dekeisha was really putting them through their paces, calling for only the most difficult cheers and strenuous gymnastics, and Beth was panting like crazy when the horn finally blew signaling halftime.

Melanie caught up with her on the way to the refreshment stand. "Great game, huh?"

Beth nodded. She didn't even know who was winning or what the score was much less whether or not it was a great game.

"Can you believe that Laura McCall?" Beth grumbled, keeping her voice low so that none of the other cheerleaders heard. "I mean, front row tickets to *Brain Damage*! We can't let her get away with that. The Fabulous Five won't have a single friend left in the world."

Melanie nodded forlornly. "Just wait until the

guys hear about it. I'll be lucky if Scott or Shane or Garrett or *anybody* ever wants to take me out again. They'll all be after Laura." Then Melanie snapped to attention and put a hand on Beth's arm. "But promise me one thing, Beth Barry. Swear that you won't come up with any more harebrained schemes to outdo Laura. Come on. *Swear!*"

Beth smiled sweetly at her friend. As a matter of fact, she had just come up with a terrific idea. Harebrained scheme? *Humpf!* she thought, but she just kept on smiling.

"Raise your hand and swear, Beth," Melanie insisted as they stopped beside the rest of the squad at the refreshment stand.

Beth slowly raised her hand. I could fake it, she thought, but then changed her mind. What's the use? she wondered, and instead of swearing, she brought her hand down across the left side of her face to wipe away some perspiration.

At that same instant Mandy McDermott, who was standing beside Beth, glanced at her. Mandy's mouth dropped open, and the next thing Beth knew, she was pointing straight at Beth's face and letting out a bloodcurdling scream.

CHAPTER

13

*B*eth stared at Mandy in surprise. "What's the matter!"

"Your face! You're bleeding!" shouted Mandy.

"Bleeding?" asked Beth incredulously.

"Oh, Beth," cried Melanie. "You've got blood all over your face!"

Beth touched her face and looked at her fingers. They were smeared with the greasepaint she had used to fake the bruises. Her sweating had made it and the Shimmering Gloss foundation run together and turn bloodred, and swiping at it had made it run all over her face.

"Quick! Call a doctor!" yelled Mandy, rushing around in circles. "Get the paramedics!" People started running toward Beth.

"Oh, my gosh! Stop her someone," Beth pleaded. She didn't want hundreds of people rushing to see her zit.

"Beth, are you hurt?" Melanie looked scared.

Beth pushed her way through the crowd and ran for the girls' room at the back of the refreshment stand. Inside, she slammed and locked the door and ran to the mirror over the sink. She stared in horror at the red makeup that had run down her face in streaks. No wonder Mandy had screamed.

Frantically Beth turned on both faucets and grabbed a handful of paper towels from the dispenser and started scrubbing the makeup off. The water ran bright red in the sink.

She took more paper towels, drying her face and patting away beads of moisture from the top of her pleated skirt. She was glad it was cardinal red. No spots showed on it.

Next she examined her face closely. She had gotten all the makeup off, but her zit stood out in proud majesty. Oh, no, she thought. What *am* I going to do? Someone was pounding on the door.

"Beth! Beth! Are you all right?" It was Melanie. "Open the door, Beth! I want to help."

Beth looked around furtively. She couldn't open the door and show her zit to the world. There were probably hundreds of people out there waiting for her. It was just like the last scene in her favorite movie, *Butch Cassidy and the Sundance Kid*, when the walls were lined with men with guns waiting for the pair to come out. Beth sighed. She only wished she could die in the same blaze of glory when she opened the door.

"Beth Barry! Answer me," Melanie insisted.

Beth spoke at the door. "I'm . . . I'm okay, Melanie. I . . . uh, the heat just got to me! Yeah! That's it. It's the heat."

"The heat? Get serious. The temperature's in the fifties, Beth," Melanie responded.

"I know . . . but the cheers. Doing the cheers with this heavy sweater on overheated me. I just need to cool off for a few minutes." Then Beth had a great idea. "Melanie," she called through the door.

"Yes, Beth."

"Do you remember the ice pack the football team put on your ankle when you sprained it during cheerleading practice?"

"Sure."

"That's what I need. I definitely need an ice pack to help me cool down. Can you get me one from Coach Bledsoe? I know he keeps them beside the team bench in case any player gets hurt."

Beth heard talking on the other side of the door. Then Melanie spoke again.

"They said they could get you one. Someone's gone after it."

Beth smiled to herself. Maybe she was going to talk her way out of this yet.

Shortly Melanie spoke again. "Beth, we've got the ice pack. Can I come in?"

"Yes," Beth answered. "You can. But no one else! And tell everyone else to go away." She cracked the door just enough for Melanie to squeeze inside, and then she locked it again quickly.

"Beth, are you sure you're all right?" Melanie asked. Beth was struck by the deep look of concern on Melanie's face.

"I'm okay. Really I am. Let me have the ice pack. How do you work it?"

"You twist it like this," said Melanie. "Apparently some chemicals mix together inside and make it cold. You do look all right. What happened to the blood on your face? I know I saw blood."

"It wasn't blood. Really. I had some theater makeup on under some flesh-toned foundation, and when I got hot doing the cheers, it started running."

"Beth Barry! You mean you scared the living daylights out of everyone over your makeup running? We thought you were in here bleeding to death."

"It's worse than bleeding to death. Look!" Beth took her hand away from the pimple she had been covering.

"Oooh," said Melanie, making a face. "That's gross."

"I knew you would say that," Beth huffed. "If I opened the door with everyone standing out there, a thousand people would have said the same thing *in unison*. I'd die. Worse yet, I wouldn't die."

"Well, you're going to have to leave here sooner or later. You can't wait until Mount Everest disappears."

Beth frowned at Melanie. "I thought it looked like Mount Everest, too, but you didn't have to say so." Then she put the ice pack against her face.

"I'm going to claim that I got too hot, and my face turned beet red. It wasn't blood everyone saw. It was just my red face and perspiration. You've got to stick up for me. Tell them that's what I looked like when you came in, but the ice pack cooled me down. I'll keep it against my face so they won't see my zit, and they'll think I'm trying to stay cool."

Melanie looked at her dubiously. "Okay, but I don't know if they'll believe it. Not after . . ."

Beth felt a stab of guilt. She knew what Melanie had started to say. Not after her big story about the fake slumber party and now everybody thought she had a super extralarge mouth. "Please, Melanie. It's so important," she began. "And I promise. I'll never ask you to do anything like this again. I *swear*!"

"Well . . . okay," Melanie relented slowly. "But just this once."

"Thanks," said Beth. "You're a real friend."

Beth sat in the grass behind the team bench and kept the ice pack against her face. She had to admit that she sort of enjoyed the attention that everyone gave her. She felt like a star, not like at home where she had to fight to get noticed. Miss Wolfe even came over to see how she was doing and told her not to do any more cheers. She also instructed the rest of the cheerleaders to take off their sweaters so they wouldn't overheat the way Beth had. Beth knew it was working perfectly when all the cheerleaders, except for Laura and Tammy, stopped by to tell her how worried they were about her. So what if I'm getting a reputation for an extralarge mouth? I'm an actress! she thought proudly, and someday I'll get an Oscar to prove it.

When Keith heard she wasn't feeling well, he left the Wakeman Warriors bench to see her, too. She moved the ice pack so that it covered both the zit and the place where the imaginary bruise was supposed to be and gazed up at him. She loved the look of concern on his face and thanked her lucky stars she had survived one more incident.

When the second half of the game started, she had time to think. The ice pack was starting to lose its coldness, but that was okay. At least it hid her pimple. On the way home she would definitely have to get some Band-Aids. She could put one on, and the next time she saw Keith she could tell him the ice pack cured her bruises. Wasn't that what you were supposed to do for bruises? she wondered. Apply ice?

Now all she had to do was figure out a way to stop

Laura McCall and her father from getting front row tickets for Brain Damage. A tiny idea was starting to form in one of the wrinkles of Beth's brain. The more she thought about it, the bigger it grew. She giggled to herself. *There was a way!*

CHAPTER

14

"Gee, Beth. Are you sure you're okay?" Keith held her hand and stared into her eyes as they sat on the Barry front porch. He had been sweet enough to walk her home rather than go to Bumpers without her.

"You'd make a *great* doctor, Keith," answered Beth. She started to flutter her eyelids at him but thought better of it. He might think it was cornball. Instead she gave him her sweetest smile, as she held the ice pack, which was by now positively warm, against her face. "You've got a great bedside manner. Or should I say *porch*side?"

Just then Todd came running out of the house and slammed the door. "Coming through!" he yelled as he leapt over them and ran down the steps. He jumped on his bike and rode off down the street doing pop-wheelies all the way.

"Is that thing still cold?" Keith asked, pointing to the ice pack.

"Oh, yes, a little. The bruises feel better with it on them. Why, I'll even bet that they'll be gone by tomorrow. I should have thought of using an ice pack before." Wow, what a stroke of genius, she thought. By Monday morning I'll be rid of my pimple, even if I have to amputate it, and he'll never know I had one. No more candy bars for me. They aren't worth it.

"It really scared me," Keith continued, "when I heard someone say you were bleeding all over the place."

"That's darling of you, Keith." She started to move the hand he wasn't holding to touch his cheek but remembered in time it was the one holding the ice pack. Instead she leaned against him and put her head on his shoulder. "You don't know how much I really like you."

He put his arm around her and held her tightly for a moment. Then he sat back and took her chin in his hand and leaned down to kiss her on the mouth. The world spun around Beth as she let her self sink against him. She felt warm all over, especially on her knees. The ice pack had sprung a leak and was dribbling all over her.

"Oh!" she said jerking back. "I've got to go in now."

"Go in?" He looked as if he couldn't believe what she was saying.

"Yes. I, uh, told my parents that I'd sit with Alicia tonight, and it's just about time for them to go out."

His face was full of disappointment. "They're going out at four-thirty on Saturday afternoon?"

"I'm sorry, Keith. Really I am." She was even sorrier that she was getting so wet and wanted to get into the house before the ice pack was completely empty and she couldn't hide behind it anymore. "I'll make it up to you. I promise," she called as she ran into the house.

Inside, it was one of those rare moments. All was quiet. Her father was watching a sports show on TV in the family room, and her mother was reading while Alicia lay on the floor in front of them coloring in a book. Agatha slept next to her. Beth could hear the dog making funny little snoring sounds. Brittany was on the phone in the hall, and Brian was probably taking a nap in preparation for another big Saturday night out.

Beth avoided a backhanded swipe by Brittany and grabbed the directory out of the telephone stand. Next she went into the family room to retrieve the entertainment section from the paper and headed upstairs to her room to work on her plan for upstaging Laura McCall. Brittany was the only one who paid any attention to her. It's as if I don't even exist around this place, Beth thought.

Darn, darn, darn, she thought. Just when things were getting super between Keith and me, that stupid ice pack had to spring a leak. She threw it viciously into the wastebasket by her desk and changed into a dry shirt and jeans.

Beth sat down and started to search through the entertainment section of the paper. Soon she found what she was looking for: an interview with Trevor Morgan, the lead musician with Brain Damage. She read through it quickly. They were going to be at the Coliseum on Friday. Where else? thought Beth. They sure wouldn't be at Bumpers. The Coliseum was the only place in town large enough to hold the crowd they would draw

After asking Trevor Morgan about his hometown of Liverpool, England, the interviewer asked, *"How would you describe Brain Damage's music, Mr. Morgan?"*

"We play rock, but not the hard stuff, you know. The secret to our success, I believe, is getting the audience involved." Beth tried to imagine the words being spoken by Trevor with his beautiful British accent. *"We like to get local people on stage, put funny clothes on them, and let them sing with the band. It helps get the audience involved."*

The interviewer asked Trevor what he liked about the United States. *"The people, of course. You've got beautiful people, love. Except you could treat your American Indians and street people a little better, you know."*

Beth skimmed the rest of the interview for information about Trevor Morgan, but there wasn't anything that everyone didn't already know.

Next she opened the directory and looked up Dekeisha Adams's number. She might as well start with her.

"Hello," answered Dekeisha.

"Hi. This is Beth."

"Oh, hi, Beth. How are you feeling?"

"Pretty good." Beth made her voice sound thin, as if maybe a blood transfusion might help. "I wanted to thank you for being concerned about me at the game, Dekeisha. That was nice of you."

"No problem," said Dekeisha. "When we saw that your face was so red, we could have sworn you were bleeding. It just goes to show you what leaping to conclusions can do."

"Yes, I guess so," Beth answered. Then she tried, with her best theatrical voice, to sound casual. "That's really something that Laura McCall's father can get front row tickets for Brain Damage's concert, isn't it?"

"Wow! It sure is."

Beth wished that Dekeisha hadn't sounded so excited. It wasn't *that* great. Well . . . maybe it was. Beth pressed on with her plan. "The only thing I know that would be even better would be to be related to someone in the Brain Damage band."

The phone was silent for a moment, and Beth wondered if Dekeisha was still there. "Related? Do you know someone who's related to one of the musicians?"

"Oh, sure," said Beth, acting surprised. "You didn't know that Jana Morgan is related to Trevor Morgan, the lead singer of Brain Damage? I thought everyone knew that."

"*I* didn't," Dekeisha said excitedly. "Wow! Have you ever met him?"

That's more like it, thought Beth. When I'm finished, everyone's going to forget about Laura's dumb old front row seats, and The Fabulous Five will be the talk of Wacko again. Next I'll call Alexis Duvall, Lisa Snow, Kim Baxter, Sara Sawyer, and . . . let's see . . . she thought, who else? I'll make a list so I don't leave anyone out, she decided.

Beth went on telling Dekeisha how Jana's ancestors had come from Liverpool, England, where Trevor Morgan's home was, and how Trevor and Jana were distant cousins. The more she talked, the easier it got, and by the time she had called everyone on her list of names, she almost believed it herself.

CHAPTER

15

"**B**ETH BARRY! How could you do such a thing?" screamed Jana. "You know I'm not related to Trevor Morgan. I've had twenty kids ask me about him already this morning, and I don't even know him. I told you that last night when you called. Why in the world did you do it?"

"Take it easy, Jana. What harm can it do if people think you're related to him? No one is going to get the chance to ask him if it's true," Beth tried to console her friend.

Beth had been walking on air all the way to school that morning. Her zit had disappeared, she was off probation with her parents, and she had called nearly everyone in the seventh grade—except The

Fantastic Foursome, of course—the night before to tell them that Jana was related to Trevor Morgan. So it was stretching the truth? So what? They had all been impressed, and Laura and her friends would absolutely curl up and die when they heard. Beth had suspected that Jana might be questioned about it before Beth saw her and had called to warn her about what she had done, emphasizing how foolproof the scheme was.

"I don't know," said Katie. "They may find out some way, and if they do, we're in *big* trouble."

"How are they going to find out?" insisted Beth.

"It worries me, too," said Christie.

"Look. Brain Damage is in town for a one-night stand at the Coliseum and one night only. They'll be gone Saturday. No one's going to find out. And just look at how famous you are, Jana, and The Fabulous Five, too. No one is talking about Laura McCall's front row seats anymore."

"She's right about that," agreed Melanie. "I've had kids I never talked to before come up to me and ask about Trevor Morgan."

"Me, too," said Christie.

"Well, I only hope you're right," said Jana. "But it scares me."

"Don't worry," said Beth. "*Nothing* can go wrong."

And nothing did go wrong for the rest of the day.

Beth felt like a celebrity with so many people stopping to ask her if it was true that Jana was related to Trevor Morgan. She basked in all the attention.

The best time was at lunch in the cafeteria when a crowd gathered around The Fabulous Five's table. Beth could see Laura McCall and The Fantastic Foursome sitting at their table all by themselves and glaring at The Fabulous Five. Beth couldn't resist smiling and waving to them. Laura looked as if she were going to explode as she whipped the end of her long braid faster and faster.

It was at Bumpers after school when lightning struck, and Beth wished she could dissolve into thin air. Kids were still crowding around The Fabulous Five, and Beth thought even Jana was beginning to enjoy the notoriety when Laura McCall came toward their booth, followed by Tammy Lucero, Melissa McConnell and Funny Hawthorne.

Laura pushed her way through the kids around the booth. "So this is the famous Jana Morgan," she said. "Is it true that you and Trevor Morgan are related?"

"Oh, I try not to drop names," said Jana. "But if that's what you've been hearing . . ."

Beth was proud of Jana's response. Who knows? she thought. She might make an actress someday herself.

"I hear you're cousins," Laura pursued the subject.

Jana looked nervous as Laura forced her into lying. "Only distant cousins," she said. She gave Beth a furtive, *you-got-me-into-this* glance.

"If you're related, he'll probably stop by your house and see your family, won't he?" continued Laura.

"Uh, he's much too busy to stop by. I suppose he'll call Mom, though."

"Isn't that nice?" said Laura sweetly to The Fantastic Foursome. Tammy, Melissa, and Funny nodded their heads obediently.

"What kind of a guy is he, Jana? Is he nice? Does he like his fans or is he stuck-up?" asked Laura.

"Oh, he's nice," said Jana. "He's not stuck-up at all, and he loves his fans. He wrote us once about how much he likes them."

Suddenly Beth smelled a rat. Where was Laura leading Jana? She wasn't asking all these questions for nothing. She tried to catch Jana's attention to warn her.

It was then that Laura asked the killer question. "Does he like you?"

"Me?" Jana answered with a laugh and a confused look on her face. "Of course he likes me. We're cousins, aren't we?"

Beth sank in the booth. She thought she knew what was coming next.

Laura grinned like a cat playing with a mouse. "If he likes you so much, why don't you ask him to come by Bumpers Friday after school and see all the fans he has here before the concert?"

"Yeah, Jana," Melissa McConnell joined in. "Why don't you ask him?"

All the kids who had been listening cheered and yelled, "YEAH, JANA! ASK HIM! ASK HIM!"

Jana's face went white. "I said he's too busy. He has to practice and set up his sound equipment and things."

Laura had caught her mouse. "He has a road crew to do that. Besides, is he too busy even to do a teensy favor for all of his fans at Bumpers? I thought you said he loves his fans."

"I did but . . ."

"Come on, Jana," Tammy Lucero said with a sly grin. "You aren't hiding something, are you?"

Jana looked as if she could die.

Beth had to help her friend. "She *will* ask him," she burst in. "And I'll bet he comes and signs autographs for everyone here."

Jana looked at Beth in shocked disbelief.

The word spread through Bumpers like wildfire. Everyone starting cheering and slapping Jana on the back and telling her what a great person she was. Only Beth sat back in silence, stunned at her own super extralarge mouth.

CHAPTER

16

"This special meeting of The Fabulous Five has been called to decide whether we're going to lynch Beth Barry or tar and feather her and run her out of town," said Jana. The Fabulous Five were in Jana's bedroom, and Beth had never seen Jana look so angry.

"I vote for tarring and feathering," said Katie. "Lynching's too fast."

"What about strangling her with one of Brain Damage's guitar strings?" asked Christie. "I can't think of anything more appropriate."

"I think we ought to make her eat her words until she bursts," volunteered Melanie.

"With her big mouth, she'd never get full," said Katie.

Beth felt as if she were falling into a bottomless pit. She had just been trying to help Jana when she told everyone at Bumpers that Jana would ask Trevor Morgan to come by and sign autographs. She hadn't even meant to say it. It had just come out that way. And then every single person in Bumpers had come over to their table to tell Jana that they couldn't wait to see Trevor Morgan in person and to get his autograph. When The Fabulous Five were finally alone, Jana had demanded an immediate meeting, and they had marched Beth to Jana's apartment.

"Beth, what were you *thinking* about?" asked Jana. She was practically in tears. "You should have known this would happen. Now what are we going to do? You know I don't know Trevor Morgan. There's no way I can get him to come to Bumpers. Except at concerts, people can't get within a hundred feet of a rock star. I'm going to look like a fool."

"The Fabulous Five are *all* going to look like fools," said Katie. "You're actually doing what The Fantastic Foursome couldn't do—make us look bad."

Beth held back tears of her own. "I'm sorry. Really I am. Every time Laura McCall made a big brag, I couldn't stand it. I just had to show her up because she was trying to show us up. Before I knew what was happening, it turned into a full-fledged bragging war."

Jana looked at her sadly for a moment. "Beth,

Beth, what are we going to do with you? Your wild stories were okay at Mark Twain Elementary where everyone knew you and how dramatic you liked to be. But people don't know you that well yet at Wakeman. They think you *mean* what you're saying. Now you've got us all in trouble. Come on, gang, think. Is there any way we can straighten this out without looking too foolish?"

"I don't know," said Christie. "You know you said that you were related to Trevor Morgan right in front of everyone, and they all heard Beth say you could get Brain Damage to come to Bumpers. It looks to me as if we're stuck."

The Fabulous Five sat around for the next half hour, gloomily trying to think up ideas that could get them out of their mess. Each time someone came up with one, the others shot holes through it. Finally the meeting broke up, and they all left dejectedly for home.

In her room Beth flung herself on her bed and lay in the dark, her eyes filled with tears. She felt almost as bad as she had the time her mother had been ill and she had thought it was her fault. She had run away and hid until her friends found her that time. If only she could do that now.

Why do I do such stupid things? Why can't I be like Melanie or Jana or Christie or Katie and know the right thing to do all the time? Even Brian and Brittany seem so sure of themselves. Every time I try to do something that people will notice, it turns out like this, a mess.

Beth rolled over onto her back and sighed. She felt like a nobody. Things had seemed so simple back at Mark Twain Elementary when they had only Taffy Sinclair to deal with. Now there was Laura and The Fantastic Foursome and everything else that was different at Wakeman Junior High.

Why have I started to feel as if there's an explosion going on inside of me with pieces flying in all directions? she wondered. All my friends are the same as before. Even as bad as the problem over Brain Damage is, they're still sticking by me. Yet there are times when everything feels different. *Why can't I control my emotions?*

Beth pulled the edge of the bedcover over her head. Her shoulders shook with sobs that she stifled in her pillow. Soon she was quiet as she slept.

The sound of Brian's music awakened her sometime later. She rubbed her eyes and wondered for a moment where she was. Her clock said six o'clock, and that meant Todd would be yelling for everyone to come to dinner shortly.

Beth got up and went into the bathroom to wash her face. She looked into the mirror and couldn't believe how bad she looked. Her hair was a mess and her eyes and nose were red.

"Suppertime!" she heard Todd yell up the stairway.

A clamor of footsteps and Agatha's barking sounded in the hall as the rest of the Barry clan ran for the kitchen. Beth dried her face, brushed on a little powder to hide the redness, and then she followed.

The conversation at the table was normal with everyone's trying to tell the story of their day and complaining about someone else's taking too much food. Agatha wandered from person to person begging hopefully for a morsel to eat.

Beth sat quietly eating, half listening to the others and passing food when asked.

"Beth, are you feeling all right?" her mother asked as she handed out dishes of blueberry cobbler for dessert. "I can't remember when you've been so quiet."

"I'm fine." She was hardly ever ill, and they all knew it.

"You don't look as if you're fine. Jeff, feel her head. Does she have a temperature?"

Everyone went silent as her father reached over and put the back of his fingers to her forehead. "Feels okay to me," he said, but he looked worried, too.

"Are you sure you're okay, Bethy?" asked Brittany.

Beth could hardly believe the looks of concern on the faces at the table. Suddenly, by not saying anything, she had become the center of attention. As hard as she had tried before, except for the time she put on the fake wounds, it had been impossible to get someone to even look at her much less listen to what she had to say.

After dinner her mother and father knocked on her door. "Honey, are you sure you're all right?" her mother asked again. "Is something wrong? Usually you're so bright and bubbly."

She reassured them she was okay, and they finally went away, but she could hear them talking in worried tones as they left. Later Alicia, Todd, Brian, and Brittany each stuck their head in the door to say something cheerful. Alicia even brought Agatha, "to cheer Bethy up," she said, and surprisingly even Brian's music was played at half its normal volume. Maybe I do amount to something in this family after all, she thought. Maybe I've just been going about things all wrong.

Her spirits lifted a tiny bit, and her mind went back to Trevor Morgan and the problem she had created for The Fabulous Five. Beth picked up the telephone directory, which she had forgotten to return to the stand in the hallway, and turned to the listing for hotels in the yellow pages.

CHAPTER

17

*B*eth ran her finger down the listings for hotels. Which one would a famous rock group stay in? The Sheraton? The Hyatt Regency? Maybe the Embassy Suites. She had heard that you got a bedroom and a living room and even a kitchen there.

She dialed the number. "Embassy Suites. May I help you?" came a pleasant voice.

"Is Brain Damage at your hotel?" Beth asked.

"Is this some kind of joke?" The voice didn't sound so pleasant this time.

"No. Brain Damage is a rock group that's in town to give a concert. I want to know if they're staying there."

"Oh," the voice sounded apologetic. "Wait a minute, please. No. There is no such listing here."

Beth thanked the voice and dialed the Sheraton. This time she explained who Brain Damage was when she asked if they were there. They weren't.

Finally she found that they were staying at the Hyatt Regency. "Could you connect me to their room?" she asked.

"They each have separate rooms, but I'm afraid I can't connect you. We have orders not to disturb them."

Beth thought quickly. "But I'm Beth Morgan, Trevor Morgan's little sister, and I need to talk to him."

"You're the fifth little sister of Trevor Morgan's who's called today. I'm afraid it won't work, honey. We have a list of specific people we can put through, and none of you little sisters are on it. Don't try delivering packages, either. Four young female delivery girls have tried that. We took the packages up to his suite on the twentieth floor for them."

Beth put down the phone in frustration. What was she going to do? It was her fault that The Fabulous Five were in trouble. It was up to her to get them out of it.

She picked up the paper that had the interview with Trevor Morgan in it and reread it. There was one idea that might work. She would talk to Miss Wolfe the first thing tomorrow.

* * *

"So you vant to borrow the Indian mascot uniform to practice for tryouts. That is very nice, Beth. I vish all the girls ver so industrious. But you must have it back in two days," said Miss Wolfe.

"Oh, thank you, Miss Wolfe," said Beth. "I'll take good care of it and definitely will have it back day after tomorrow. I really want a chance to be the Wakeman Warrior at the football games."

Beth took the brightly colored Indian mascot costume with its beautiful war bonnet with red-tipped feathers and put it in her locker. Her idea had to work. It just had to. The Fabulous Five had been walking around with a look of doom all day, and it got deeper during lunch period when people crowded around their table to tell Jana how super she was and to ask when Trevor Morgan was going to be at Bumpers. Jana had just said she didn't know yet and had thrown angry looks at Beth. Beth's telling them that she was doing everything she could to reach Trevor and invite him to Bumpers hadn't made a difference.

Worse yet, every time Beth looked at The Fantastic Foursome's table she saw Laura smiling at them. Laura must have guessed that she really had The Fabulous Five trapped this time, and she was going to enjoy every minute of it.

Beth slipped into the elevator. She had put on the Indian costume over the jeans she was wearing in the ladies' room and had used her lipstick to put streaks like war paint on her forehead and cheeks. She also ran a red line down the center of her nose for good measure. Then she had peeked out the door until there were no hotel employees in sight and run to the elevator.

She excused herself to the older couple who got on with her and punched the button for the twentieth floor. That was the floor the woman on the switchboard had mentioned when Beth talked to her. Beth hoped it hadn't been a lie they used to confuse people who might want to sneak in to see Trevor Morgan. The man and the woman stared at her until they got off at the fourteenth floor.

Beth watched the lighted numbers change from seventeen to eighteen to nineteen. She took a deep breath as the elevator stopped at the twentieth floor. The doors opened and she stepped into a beautiful, marble-floored foyer with potted plants on both sides. In front of her were two huge doors that were as pretty as the doors on the cathedral downtown, except they were smaller.

She brushed the wrinkles out of the costume and straightened the war bonnet on her head. Then she walked forward carefully, listening for the sound of rock music. It was quiet.

She stepped up to the doors and hesitated with her finger over the bell button. Should she really go through with this? What if she was so nervous she forgot what she wanted to say? How could she think like that? She was going to be an actress, wasn't she? She would act as if she were playing the starring role in a big Broadway play and Trevor Morgan was a costar. Beth punched the button hard and straightened her bonnet one more time.

The door opened and Trevor Morgan stood before her in just a pair of old sweat pants. His dark hair, the same color as Jana's, hung to his shoulders, and Beth couldn't help thinking that they could actually pass for cousins. "I say, what have we here? It's a bloomin' Indian. Can I help you, luv?"

"Er, uh . . . yes, Mr. Morgan. My name is Little Fawn. Well, actually it's Beth Barry, but my Indian name is Little Fawn, you see." Beth had her fingers crossed behind her back even though she hadn't told a lie yet. Her name was Little Fawn when she belonged to Indian Princesses back in third grade, and she had a framed certificate on her bedroom wall to prove it.

"I belong to the Cherokee tribe," she went on. "I saw in the paper that you were interested in American Indians, and I thought I'd come and tell you about us."

Trevor looked at her in amazement, then he stepped back and made a gallant gesture for her to enter.

Beth had never seen such a beautiful room. It was filled with luxurious furniture, and an electric guitar was set up, and sheet music was spread all over the floor. One whole wall was glass, and she could see way out over the city. This is the way I'm going to live when I'm a star, she thought. "Wow!" she said, and clamped a hand over her mouth.

"Kind of like it, do ya?" Trevor asked. "It is a bit of a good view, if I do say so meself. Can I get you a soda or something?"

Beth shook herself to clear her head, and the war bonnet slipped down over one ear. She straightened it and said, "Oh, no. Thank you very much, though."

"Well," said Trevor, "have a seat then and tell me about yourself and your tribe. I want to hear all about it."

Beth sat down on a sofa which was so big that when she scooted all the way back her feet stuck straight out. "Well, let's see," she said. "What do you want to know?" She had decided to let *him* tell her what he wanted to know. That way her super extra-large mouth wouldn't get her into as much trouble.

"Tell me about your tribe. Is it on one of those reservations? And how big is it?"

"No. It's not on a reservation. Not all Indians live on reservations." Beth was sure about that since she remembered it from her history class. "They live all over the United States."

"They do?" He seemed really surprised to hear that.

"Yes, and my tribe was, er, *is* small. The last time I counted there were twenty-two of us."

"And do you get along well in this country?" he asked.

"Yes, I do," she answered. "I go to school at Wakeman Junior High right here in town and have lots of friends. I know some Indians don't get along as well as we do, though. The kids at Wakeman are kind of special."

"I'm glad to hear that. You're a real luv, you are."

Beth knew that her chance had just arrived. If she were going to get The Fabulous Five out of trouble, it would be *right now.* "I wonder if you could maybe help me thank the kids at Wakeman for being so nice to me?" she asked.

"How's that?"

"Well, they have a special place they hang out. It's called Bumpers. You'd like it if you saw it. It's decorated with old bumper cars from amusement park rides, and it has an ancient Wurlitzer jukebox." Beth stopped to catch her breath. She was getting off the subject. "I know it's asking an awful lot, and you probably can't do it," she said softly, putting on her best poor-little-girl look, "but if you could maybe stop by there . . ."

Trevor Morgan frowned at her.

He knows I'm putting him on, Beth thought. *I'm dead.*

"I'm really sorry," Trevor said. "But me schedule won't allow for it."

Beth's spirits dove to the soles of her feet. She was ruined.

"But I've got another idea, luv. Do ya want to hear it?"

CHAPTER

18

The Coliseum was packed with kids as Beth and
the rest of The Fabulous Five squeezed through the
people already sitting in the row where their seats
were located. The noise almost made Beth wish she
had brought the earplugs she used for swimming.

She couldn't wait for the concert to begin so she
could hear Trevor Morgan and Brain Damage per-
form. He hadn't been able to come to Bumpers, but
his plan had been even better than hers.

"Hi, Jana and everybody," called Marcie Bee. "Is
Trevor coming to Bumpers after the concert?"

"You'll just have to wait and see," Jana shouted
back above the noise. She looked at Beth and smiled.
Jana, Christie, Katie, and Melanie had loved the

plan, too, and had forgiven Beth for getting them
into so much trouble.

"Oh, look, there are Laura, Tammy, Melissa, and
Funny," said Melanie to the others. They were going
into the first row just as Laura had said. "And
they've got Alexis, Mandy, Dekeisha, and some of
the other girls with them."

"Laura must have gotten them tickets," said Katie. "They see us. Let's wave and smile really big."

The Fabulous Five stuck their hands up and
waved at The Fantastic Foursome. Laura, who was
leading the way, saw them and frowned.

"Wow! I'll bet she's wondering what's going on
now," said Christie.

"Let her wonder. She'll suffer later," said Jana.

The lights dimmed, and the warm-up band came
on. It was a local group, and the crowd didn't quiet
down very much for them.

Beth spotted Keith two rows over and waved to
him. He nudged Scott and Randy, who saw them
and waved. Clarence Marshall was throwing pop-
corn at everyone.

Finally, after what seemed an eternity, the master
of ceremonies came back on and the local band left.

"GUYS AND GIRLS," he called over the public
address system. "THE FEATURED ATTRAC-
TION FOR THIS EVENING, THE GROUP
THAT YOU'VE ALL BEEN WAITING FOR,
BEING BROUGHT TO YOU ALL THE WAY

FROM LONDON, ENGLAND . . ."—he paused for effect—"I GIVE YOU THAT INCOMPARABLE BAND . . . *BRAIN DAMAGE!*" The crowd roared as Trevor Morgan jumped onto the stage in black pants with silver stripes running down the sides. His shirt was black with silver studding, and the front was opened down to his belt. His black boots flared all the way up to his knees, and his hair stuck out in spikes.

The other members of Brain Damage followed him out, jumping wildly. They were dressed in all kinds of wild costumes. Their faces were made up like clowns, creatures from outer space, and things Beth couldn't describe.

For the next two hours Brain Damage played nonstop, and the kids jumped up and down and rocked back and forth, screaming all the time. Beth and her friends screamed right along and pounded each other during the parts they liked best.

When Brain Damage started playing slowly, Beth knew they were getting near the end of the concert. She crossed her fingers and prayed that Trevor wouldn't forget her. After two hours of playing the way they had, she didn't know how he could remember anything.

Trevor Morgan stepped to the microphone. His voice sounded raspy, as if he were about to lose it.

"Oh, please don't get laryngitis now," Beth said out loud.

"I want to take a moment to thank you all," said Trevor. "You've been a wonderful audience, you really have, luvs." He pulled a small piece of paper from his belt.

Beth recognized it and punched Katie and Jana, who were standing next to her. The Fabulous Five all doubled up their fists and bounced on their toes in pent-up excitement.

"I want to thank the kids from Wakeman Junior High—I hear you call it Wacko—and say hello to my good friends Jana Morgan, Christie Winchell, Katie Shannon, and Melanie Edwards. I hear you're nice to Indians. And of course, I can't forget my very good friend Beth Barry. I love you all and wish I could stop by Bumpers, but you know how show business is."

The Fabulous Five jumped straight up in the air and screamed. Beth had never felt so wonderful. He had done just what he had said he would do.

Then Trevor held up his hand for silence again. "As you know, we always pick someone from the audience to join us on stage, and so for our very last number, I'm going to ask another group to come up right now. A group you're going to love as much as I do. *The Fabulous Five!*"

Suddenly sirens went off and spotlights beamed down on them out of nowhere, and before any of the girls knew what was happening, the members of Brain Damage were rushing them onto the stage.

Trevor Morgan grabbed Beth's hand and pulled her up the stairs, grinning back over his shoulder at her. She felt a hat plop onto her head and a microphone being thrust into her hand.

"Sing your heart out, luv!" Trevor shouted. "You're a *STAR*!"

Beth clutched the mike and started singing to the familiar tune of a Brain Damage hit. Out of the corners of her eyes she could see her best friends singing, too, while the members of the band pranced around the stage. Over the blare of the music the crowd roared its appreciation. It was all too wonderful to be true.

Beth stood back until Jana, Melanie, Katie, and Christie had finished talking to Trevor in his dressing room. He had told Beth that he wanted to see all of them after the performance.

"It's been nice meeting you all," said Trevor as they started leaving. "Keep up the good work with those Indians now."

Beth hung back. Now that she knew Trevor so well, and he had even let her sing onstage, maybe he would give her a real audition with his band if she asked him. Other kids her age had made it big.

"Trevor, I can't tell you how much I appreciate what you've done," she told him, putting on her most mature face. Would he think she looked like Madonna?

"No problem, luv. It's been my pleasure, really. Matter of fact, it's been a pleasant change from young girls trying to sneak into my apartment and ask me for an audition. And it's been real refreshing meeting a real live American Indian." He turned and started rubbing makeup off his face.

"Oh . . ." said Beth weakly. That shot that. There was no way she could ask him for a real audition now. And besides, she was feeling very guilty about telling him she was an Indian when she really truly wasn't one. It was one thing to try and outbrag Laura McCall, but it was something else to lie to such a nice person as Trevor.

"Trevor," she said meekly.

"Yes," he answered as two men came into the dressing room and started collecting his guitar and other equipment.

"I have to tell you something."

"What's that?" he asked. He was hurrying now.

"I'm not a true Indian." There, she had said it.

He stopped and looked at her. Then he smiled and said, "That doesn't surprise me. I've heard about people being part Indian. I guess it's hard to be full-blooded Indian these days what with all the intermarriage. I think that speaks well for you Yanks. Now, if you'll excuse me, I've got to get changed. We've got to be in Boston tomorrow."

Beth nodded. She started toward the door to make her exit, but then stopped. Tingles tiptoed up the back of her neck. She still hadn't been honest with him, she thought. Not really. Oh, sure, she reasoned. She had tried, but he still had the wrong impression. He thought she was a heroine!

She turned around again, praying silently that he hadn't already started to undress. He hadn't, but from his expression she could see that he was getting anxious for her to leave.

"What I mean is, I'm not *any* kind of Indian," she began. "I read in the newspaper that you are concerned about American Indians and the homeless, so I borrowed an Indian costume from school. It was just a trick to get to meet you, and now I'm sorry. *Not that I met you*!" she added quickly. "Sorry that I tricked you."

Trevor stroked his chin and regarded her solemnly. "So, you tricked Trevor Morgan, did you?" he asked.

The stern sound in his voice made her stomach flip-flop. "Yes, sir," she murmured, feeling only two inches tall. What did he think of her now? What was he going to say?

Suddenly his face brightened. "Well, I won't admit it to anyone if you promise you won't!"

Beth's eyes popped open. "You won't?" she stammered, feeling giddy with relief. "I mean, *I* won't! I promise!" She kept right on talking as she backed toward the door. "Wow! Thanks a lot!"

"Wait," he said. "There's one more thing."

Beth froze to the stop. Her mind was racing. *What now?*

"I want you to spend some time finding out about *real* Indians, luv," he said quietly. "I'll bet you could even think of some ways to help them if you tried."

"I will. I'll do everything I can. Honest," Beth assured him, and she had never felt more sincere in her life.

CHAPTER

19

"Okay, Beth Barry, repeat after me," said Jana. The Fabulous Five were meeting in Jana's room on the Saturday afternoon after the concert, just as they had when they were in Mark Twain Elementary. Beth was facing her four friends and had her right hand in the air. "I, Beth Barry, do solemnly swear . . ."

Beth repeated the words. "I, Beth Barry, do solemnly swear . . ."

"That I will not tell any more wild stories. . ." continued Jana.

"That I will not tell any more wild stories. . ." answered Beth.

"That will in any way make my friends look dumb," said Jana.

"That will in any way make my friends look dumb," Beth finished the oath. Her left hand was behind her where her friends couldn't see it, and her fingers were crossed. After all, she reasoned, if she hadn't told Trevor Morgan that she was an Indian, The Fabulous Five would never have gotten to go on stage and sing with Brain Damage and win the bragging war with Laura McCall.

"Okay, everybody, I think we have now gotten through to Beth. She may have finally learned her lesson," said Jana. The four of them gathered around Beth and hugged her.

"Please, stay out of trouble," said Christie. "You're such a cute kid, you don't need to tell stories to get attention."

"That's right," agreed Katie. "We love you just the way you are, big mouth and all, but we can do without your stories."

Beth stuck her tongue out at Katie. "My Indian story did turn out pretty great, didn't it?"

"Yeah," said Jana, "Score a big one for The Fabulous Five. Did you see the faces of Laura and her friends when Trevor had us up on the stage? I thought Laura was going to burst into flames."

"I did, too," said Melanie.

"When all's said and done, Beth, I guess you did pull it out," Christie admitted.

"Terrific," said Beth and a sly smile slowly spread

across her face. "And now that we've settled that, I want to talk to you about the plight of the American Indians."

CHAPTER

20

*J*ana sank into her seat in family living class just as the final bell rang. She was breathless from running because she had stopped between classes to tell her friend Funny Hawthorne that she was going to be maid of honor at the wedding of her mother and Pink in two weeks. She had tried her best to sound happy about the wedding—happier than she really felt.

Mrs. Clark was calling the class to attention. "Boys and girls," she was saying. "I'm pleased to announce that you are all about to become parents."

Jana stared openmouthed at her teacher. Around her, other kids giggled or made gasping sounds.

"That's right," said Mrs. Clark in response to their surprise. "Each one of you is going to be mother or father to a darling baby and learn what it's like to have the responsibilities of parenthood. You may decide to be a single parent, or pair up with someone in this class so that your baby will have both a mother and a father and you will have someone to share that responsibility with. But it must be someone from *this* class, not Mrs. Blankenship's class, because you'll be graded together on the project."

Rats! thought Jana. That meant she couldn't be partners with her boyfriend, Randy Kirwan, because he was in Mrs. Blankenship's class. She had dreamed so many times of their getting married when they grew up and having kids of their own.

"The choice is up to you," Mrs. Clark went on. "But whichever decision you make, you must bring a stuffed animal or doll to class Wednesday to be approved as your child and begin treating it as if it were a real baby."

"I'm not going to change any diapers," yelled Richie Corrierro from the back of the room.

"Oh, yes, you are," Mrs. Clark corrected him. "At least three times a day, but I'll explain more about your jobs as parents when you bring in your children on Wednesday. Between now and then, be thinking about choosing your children and your partners."

Jana sank back in her chair. *Parents*, she thought. That was suddenly becoming the most important word in her vocabulary. Her mother was getting married in two weeks, and she was going to have a stepfather. Did that mean she would never get to see her natural father again? And now she was going to have a baby of her own to take care of, and she couldn't be parents with Randy because he was in another class. Would all of it be too much for her to handle? Find out in *The Fabulous Five #6: The Parent Game*.

ABOUT THE AUTHOR

Betsy Haynes, the daughter of a former news-woman, began scribbling poetry and short stories as soon as she learned to write. A serious writing career, however, had to wait until after her marriage and the arrival of her two children. But that early practice must have paid off, for within three months Mrs. Haynes had sold her first story. In addition to a number of magazine short stories and the Taffy Sinclair series, Mrs. Haynes is also the author of *The Great Mom Swap* and its sequel, *The Great Boyfriend Trap.* She lives in Colleyville, Texas, with her children and husband, a businessman who is also an author.

Great FREE offer just for you!

Join SNEAK PEEKS™!

Do you want to know what's new before anyone else? Do you like to read great books about girls just like you? If you do, then you won't want to miss SNEAK PEEKS™! Be the first of your friends to know what's hot ... When you join SNEAK PEEKS™, we'll send you FREE inside information in the mail about the latest books ... *before they're published!* Plus updates on your favorite series, authors, and exciting new stories filled with friendship and fun ... adventure and mystery ... girlfriends and boyfriends.

It's easy to be a member of SNEAK PEEKS™. Just fill out the coupon below ... and get ready for fun! It's FREE! Don't delay—sign up today!